Books by Bill Wallace

Red Dog
Trapped in Death Cave

Available From ARCHWAY Paperbacks

Beauty
The Biggest Klutz in Fifth Grade
Blackwater Swamp
Buffalo Gal
The Christmas Spurs
Danger in Quicksand Swamp
Danger on Panther Peak
   (Original title: Shadow on the Snow)
A Dog Called Kitty
Ferret in the Bedroom, Lizards in the Fridge
The Final Freedom
Journey into Terror
Never Say Quit
Snot Stew
Totally Disgusting!
True Friends
Watchdog and the Coyotes

Available from MINSTREL Books

BILL WALLACE

THE FINAL FREEDOM

A MINSTREL® HARDCOVER
PUBLISHED BY POCKET BOOKS
New York London Toronto Sydney Tokyo Singapore

A MINSTREL HARDCOVER

 A Minstrel Book published by
POCKET BOOKS, a division of Simon & Schuster Inc.
1230 Avenue of the Americas, New York, NY 10020

Wallace, Bill, 1947–
    The final freedom / Bill Wallace.
        p. cm.
    Summary: When thirteen-year-old Will Burke and the famed Apache chief Geronimo forge a unique bond of friendship, each wins a special kind of freedom.
    ISBN 0-671-52999-4
    [1. Friendship—Fiction. 2. Freedom—Fiction. 3. Geronimo, 1829–1909—Fiction. 4. Apache Indians—Fiction. 5. Indians of North America—Fiction.] I. Title.
PZ7.W15473Fi 1997
[Fic]—dc20   96-28424
                                                    CIP
                                                    AC

First Minstrel Books hardcover printing February 1997

10 9 8 7 6 5 4 3 2

A MINSTREL BOOK and colophon are registered trademarks of Simon & Schuster Inc.

Printed in the U.S.A.

*In memory of William Thomas
and Elgia Estella Burke*

PROLOGUE

The woman was Indian, but she did not understand Apache. Nor was there any sign of recognition in her eyes when he spoke to her in Spanish—the tongue of the hated Mexicans to the south. She only stared at the body of her man, not blinking as she clutched her baby.

The brave who led the raiding party had never spoken English before a White. He knew the tongue well, but had always gained more by pretending he did not. And although this woman was Indian—regardless of her tribe, she was *not* Indian. She had left the Indian way by marrying this White. That made her a White.

He stared down at her and thoughtfully stroked a hand over his weathered, pitted cheek. Then he sighed.

"I have fought and killed many brave warriors," he said in English.

The woman blinked and glanced away from her man

for only an instant. It was enough for him to know that she understood.

"I have never done battle with one such as your man. With his seed he gave you a son—now his spirit and courage have given life to the son a second time. You and the baby will not be harmed."

She gave a nod, but it was so slight that only the sharpest eye could catch it. The brave turned to the three others who stood beside him.

"Leave a horse and food for the woman," he ordered in Apache. "We must go."

After the men turned, he reached down and pulled the gun from beneath the lifeless body at his feet. A lone eagle feather adorned the war shaman's headband. He took it and tied it to the barrel of the gun with a thin strip of rawhide. He then wrapped his headband around the woman's arm where a bullet had ripped her skin.

The braves hobbled a horse with rawhide bands so it could not follow when they thundered off.

The shaman took one last look at the courageous warrior, the woman, and the boy. The child had the eyes of his father—blue-gray, like the sky seen through an early morning mist. Perhaps, the warrior thought, he will have the heart as well. With one fluid sweep he grabbed a clump of mane and swung his left leg over the tall sorrel gelding that he had chosen for his own.

"We will sing of this battle and of your man. What was his name?"

He expected the woman to whisper with her eyes

cast to the ground. Perhaps she would not even answer. Instead, she raised her head and stared at him proud and defiant.

"Jesse Hunt." Her voice was loud—full of her man's strength and courage.

"The name Jesse Hunt will be sung around our campfires. His weapon will have a place of honor in my lodge. He will be a legend among the Apache."

Pushed by a soft southern breeze, the eagle feather gently swayed from the barrel of the gun. Not a rifle, not a shotgun, the weapon was a thing to be cherished. He clutched it to his chest, just as the woman clutched the baby to hers. Then he spun his horse and galloped away, across a dry, dusty land.

For months he had longed for this taste of freedom. He had hoped it would last forever. Freedom had been sweet. Now, with only three men and himself, he had no choice but to return. Return to San Carlos. Return to the anger of the White soldiers. Return to the sour meat that crawled with maggots and the flour that moved and seemed alive with meal worms. This third escape had been far too short. But four braves could not make a raiding party. Not even four Apache. With a sigh he vowed that this escape would not be his last.

CHAPTER 1

The wood on the boardwalk felt cold beneath my bare feet.

That first week of October, in 1903, had been a regular "record breaker." Not only in the Oklahoma Territory, just to the west of us, but right here in Rush Springs, Indian Territory. Most all of both Territories had suffered a hard freeze. October was a mite too early for any kind of freeze, much less a hard one. But things were fast getting back to normal for this time of year. Yesterday the sun had come out, and this morning was starting up warm and pretty as could be. The red dirt had been almost comfortable to walk barefoot. But the boardwalk, nestled beneath the awning of Nash's Mercantile, hadn't been touched yet by the warmth of the sun.

Just as I reached to push open the screen door, the

turkey bell that hung inside jingled. Cotton Nash and Nate Ferguson stepped into the open doorway. They stood there, staring at me. It was probably only an instant, but it seemed like we stood there forever. Finally I moved aside. Nate smiled.

The bell jingled as the door bounced shut behind them. Cotton looked around his friend at me.

"Headed to the depot? Train should be in any time now."

I shook my head. "Got to fetch Mama some groceries first. Soon as I get that done . . ." I tried to squeeze between Nate and the doorway. He folded his arms, sneered down his pointed nose at me, and leaned against the door so I couldn't get through.

"You don't want to miss the train," Cotton went on. "This is the biggest thing that's happened around here, *ever.* I mean, Miss Potts even let school out. She don't never do that—not for nothin'."

I stepped in the other direction, trying to get between Nate and Cotton. Nate just rocked to his left. His shoulder almost touched Cotton's, and there wasn't room to squeeze through. I backed away. There was no sense pushing it.

Finally Cotton nudged his friend with an elbow.

"Let's go, Nate. I bet most everybody in town is down there already. Don't want to be late." He started off down the boardwalk. "Better hurry, Will," he called over his shoulder. "Don't want to miss the goings-on."

Nate stood there, glaring at me for a moment before he spun and followed Cotton.

"Bet ya two bits he don't show up at the depot,"

Nate said—making sure it was loud enough for me to hear. "He's part Injun, ya know. Bet he's scared them soldiers will mistake him for one of the savages and drag him off to the reservation at Fort Sill."

Both boys laughed. The sound echoed in my ears long after they had jumped from the boardwalk and trotted down the street toward the depot.

My fist was clenched at my side. I forced it to open and stared down at my trembling hand. "One of these days, Nate Ferguson—one of these days . . ."

My eyes left the two boys and drifted toward the window in front of the Mercantile. Quickly I made myself push the screen door open. "Don't have time for dreaming," I scolded myself. "Don't look at that window. You got to take the stuff to Mama so you can get to the depot. That'll show that stinky Nate Ferguson you ain't scared. It'll prove to him . . ."

The turkey bell jingled over my head, and the screen door bounced shut behind me.

"I hear this makes the fifteenth time they caught him and brought him back to the reservation." Ben Nash glanced up from his tally book. "Don't it?"

Chauncy Karlton leaned over the counter to make sure Ben's addition on the tally sheet wasn't getting away from him.

"Fifteen sounds about right. Shoot, I was here back in ninety-four when they brought him and the rest of the Apache in from Fort Marion, the reservation where they put them down in Florida. Told folks that the old rascal wouldn't stay put."

"I hear tell that he's got ninety-nine scalps on a pole back in his tepee." Ben leaned across the counter. "They say he's swore he'll get a hundred 'fore he dies."

Chauncy nodded. "Heard the same story—ninety-nine scalps."

"Reckon it's true?" Ben asked.

"Ninety-nine is a powerful big number," Chauncy scoffed with a wave of his hand. "This time Geronimo took a couple of young bucks and snuck off, clean to the Texas line 'fore they catched him. They didn't kill nobody, like they used to back in the old days. But there ain't no such thing as a tame Apache. Now, I think ninety-nine scalps is probably an exaggeration. But you mark my word, that scamp will take off again. And if he does have ninety-nine scalps, you can bet your life he'll make it a hundred before he dies."

Ben nodded and grunted his agreement. Chauncy watched him writing numbers on the tally sheet like a hawk would watch a field mouse.

"Back in the old days," Chauncy continued, leaning farther over the counter, "it was a lot bigger goings-on. Newspapermen and small-time politicians and folks like that would come flockin' in when he was caught. Hear that this time there's only a couple of boys from the local paper up in Guthrie. Guess it ain't no big deal no more. I mean, he ain't nothin' but an old drunk nowadays."

"Still news in the East." Ben never looked up from his addition. "Still writing stories about him. Think if he takes a deep breath, somebody would write about it. Hi, Will." Ben Nash stopped talking just long enough to nod at me, then went right back to his conversation. "Reckon he's got them scalps stashed someplace or right out in the open?"

Chauncy started to answer, then stopped to tap a finger at one of Ben's numbers. "What's that for?"

Nervously Ben glanced around the room as if he was trying to make sure nobody was listening.

"Three yards of cotton print."

Chauncy frowned. "What for you charging me for three yards of cotton?"

Ben's eyes sort of rolled around in his head. "Emma bought three yards of cotton print, day 'fore yesterday."

Chauncy frowned and folded his arms.

"I don't 'member seein' it round the house."

Ben scanned the room once more.

"You ain't supposed to know about it, you snoopy ole coot. It's for you, a new shirt." Ben's whisper was almost a growl. "She didn't figure you'd come in till next week to settle your account and . . ."

Chauncy smiled. He kind of rocked back and laced his thumbs under the straps of his bib overalls. "Makin' me a new shirt for my birthday, ain't she?"

Ben glared at him and put a finger to his lips.

"It's a nightshirt, and it's supposed to be a surprise, Chauncy. Emma finds out you know about it, she'll have my hide. Now, I mean it! Don't you let on or Emma will . . ."

Impatiently I shifted from one foot to the other. I

wished they'd stop their yammering so I could get my stuff and be on my way. Chauncy laid some money on the counter to settle up his account. While Mr. Nash was making change, the sound of a distant train whistle made all three of us look toward the door of Nash's Mercantile.

"Thanks." Chauncy smiled, taking his change from the counter. "Got to get down to the depot. See you fellas later."

Mr. Nash watched him leave, then turned his attention to me.

"How come you ain't at the depot, Will? Cotton and all the rest of the kids in town are down there."

I shrugged. "Daddy's supposed to be there. Took off work early to come down from Chickasha, but Mama needed supplies for the hotel 'fore I can go. She reckoned there might be a few folks comin' in on the train and sent me to fetch some stuff."

Mr. Nash nodded. "Okay, what'll it be?"

I closed my eyes, searching the list I'd made in my head.

"Need five pounds of sugar, pound of salt, some black pepper, and one of them mills—Mama said a small one, for puttin' on the table—two pounds of tea, and . . . and . . ." I squeezed my eyes tighter and bit my lip. "What was that?— Oh, yeah, four pounds of coffee."

Mr. Nash brought my things for me and put them in a wooden box. "Dad said put it on our bill." He nodded. I tucked the box under my right arm. As I walked through the door, I put my left hand up alongside my face—like blinders on a mule. With my hand shielding my eyes, I wouldn't be tempted to look. I wouldn't have to see it and dream about it and get myself all worked up again. Besides, I had to hurry if I was going to see Geronimo.

CHAPTER 2

Once on the boardwalk, past the front window of the Mercantile and past temptation, I took my left hand down from the side of my head and held the box. With both hands on the thing, I could run. I took off.

It was two blocks down the street to our three-story brick hotel. The train whistle tooted again. It was closer than when I heard it from inside the Mercantile, but still not to the depot. With luck, there was time for me to get the supplies home and run back to the other end of town before all the excitement was over.

I ran harder.

Mama was in the kitchen when I flew through the back door, set the box on the table, and spun to make my escape. Right as the screen bounced shut behind me, I heard her voice.

"Will? Where's the flour?"

My ears and head heard her call, but it took my feet three more strides before they got the message.

"Will?"

I stopped dead in my tracks and turned. She opened the screen door and cocked an eyebrow.

"I've got to have the flour."

"But, Mama." The whiney words that came out of my mouth sounded more like those of a little kid than a practically grown twelve-year-old man. "Can't I bring it after—"

"I must start the dough now, or there will be no bread for our guests tonight."

"But, Mama . . ." I pleaded.

She folded her arms. "I'm sorry."

"Oh, all right." I jerked around and kicked at a clump of dirt. A sudden, sharp pain raced from my big toe to my knee. I thought my kneecap was going to explode. From there, the pain shot to my hip, then up my spine to throb at the back of my skull. I had to clamp my lips together to keep from squealing like a little baby.

A rock lay half hidden beneath the clump of dirt. Blood trickled from my big toe. You dumb, stupid . . .

"Need a jar of blackstrap molasses, too," Mama called. It took my thoughts away from all the bad names I was trying to come up with for myself.

I didn't bother to turn around. I simply nodded and limped on my way. By the time I reached the road, dust had coated the scraped toe and the blood had clotted. When I got to the end of the block where our hotel stood, I didn't even notice the pain. Fact was, my pride was about the only thing that still hurt.

"No wonder you can't get a real job," I muttered at myself. "Want people to treat you like you're grown up, but shoot—only a kid would go around kickin' rocks barefooted. Next time I go down to Ferguson's Mill or over to Thompson's to ask about gettin' a job, I'm wearin' shoes!"

The sound of the train whistle made me glance up from my dusty feet. I saw the stream of gray-black smoke that puffed up from behind the little depot at the far end of town. "No sense rushing now, Will." I sighed and looked back at my dusty feet again. "You've missed all the excitement."

Then a little smile tugged at the corners of my mouth. "No sense rushing . . ." I repeated. "That means I got time to look in the window at the Mercantile." My pace quickened. Before I knew it, I was running. I jumped from the street to the boardwalk and didn't slow until I passed Nash's front door. Like a bird dog on point, I froze motionless before the window. It was still there. The smile stretched my face so much that I could see my teeth reflecting as tiny dots of white against the store window.

I had been there when Ben Nash and his boy, Cotton, had pulled the .410 shotgun from the crate. I had been one of the first people to see it when they held it up, all shiny and new and covered with grease. It was the most beautiful gun I'd ever seen.

It was a Winchester. A double barrel with carving

on the sides. Etched in the metal was a picture of hounds chasing after a big buck deer. Around that were scrolls and curlicues and swirls for decoration. Even the two hammers were etched to give them a rough surface, making it easier to cock. The stock was solid walnut—a rich dark color that shined, slick and pretty as could be.

Ben Nash had ordered it for Lester Ferguson as a Christmas present for his son. But when it didn't arrive before Christmas, Lester bought Nate another shotgun. Anyhow, that's what Cotton had told me the day I went for groceries and saw them opening the box.

The moment I got home, I told Mama and Daddy about it. I'd wanted it so badly, my insides hurt. But the gun cost fifteen dollars, and Daddy didn't have that much. Times were hard and the hotel, though busy, wasn't completely full. I remembered the pocketknife, it was called a Pocket Hunter, and it had two blades and a yellow handle. And I remembered the cat's-eye marbles. I'd wanted them and begged and pestered and reminded Mama and Daddy until they finally gave in and got them.

But that was different. Back then I was a little kid. Now I was twelve years old. That was might near grown. And when you're might near a grown man . . . well . . . you don't go around whimpering and begging your mama and daddy for stuff.

The next day I'd asked Ben Nash about buying the shotgun, or at least having him put it back until I could get a job and make enough money to pay for it. Ben agreed—sort of. "Soon as you get a job," he'd said,

"I'll put her in the back room. 'Less you got a job, though, I got to keep her in the front window and try to sell her. Times is hard. Can't keep stuff hid away when there's a chance it might sell. I'm a business-man."

It was in January when I'd talked to Ben Nash about the shotgun. Between school and chores around the hotel there was hardly time to find a job. Whenever I asked, folks would say: "Times are hard. Ain't no sense hiring a kid when grown men are begging for work. Come back later."

Now it *was* later. It was October—a whole lifetime had come and gone since I first saw the gun. And with October, with fall, people thought more about hunting. There were passenger pigeons, quail, dove, and rabbits, and the older boys at school were all the time going out hunting on Saturdays. If I could only have me that shotgun . . . If I could get good at hittin' birds, that'd show them. That would prove to Nate and the others that I was just like them. I was just as good. If I could hunt with them, it'd show them that I really did fit in.

I traced my tongue over my teeth. They felt dry and rough. I closed my mouth, chased the silly smile from my face, and forced the memories and dreams from my head. I blinked and tore my eyes from the shotgun. It was only a matter of time before I'd pass this store window and the gun of my dreams would be gone for-ever. My bare feet dragged on the boardwalk as I moved to open the door.

CHAPTER 3

Mr. Nash was on the ladder, stacking cans on one of the top shelves. When the turkey bell above the door jingled, he glanced over his shoulder.

"Will, what you doin' back here, boy? Way you lit out, I figured you was gonna dump them groceries and hightail it down to the depot. You forget somethin'?"

"Yes, sir." My mouth was still dry from standing outside, grinning and dreaming over that dumb shotgun. I swallowed and cleared my throat. "I forgot flour. And Mama needs a can of blackstrap molasses."

"Fetch me them five things of green beans." Mr. Nash pointed at the counter. "Soon as I get them stacked, I'll bring your stuff."

I stepped behind the counter and lifted the cans to him, one at a time. He shoved them into the open space on the shelf and climbed down. "Ten pounds of flour or twenty?"

"Reckon she'll need twenty. We got about six rail hands staying in the third-floor commons. She and Daddy are figurin' there might be a couple of fellas comin' in on the train with them Apache, too."

Mr. Nash spun and waddled toward the storeroom. It took him only a moment or two to return with the white cotton sack of flour. I leaned my right shoulder toward him and he lifted it—held on until he was sure I had it balanced.

"Be mighty careful with that," he cautioned. "Lester Ferguson done went and stuffed a whole bunch of flour into that thin little cotton sack. That cotton's so thin it looks like cheesecloth. Ferguson's gettin' tight in his old age. Used to sack in thick cotton."

The sack was heavy. I nodded and adjusted it on my shoulder. Made sure I had a good hold on it.

"Ain't got no can of molasses," he said. I could hardly hear him when he turned and bent down behind the cabinet. "Last shipment that came, they put the molasses in these little glass jars." He straightened and handed it over the counter to me as gingerly as Mother handled her fine china dishes. "Might ought to be careful with this, too," he said. "Ain't a good heavy bell jar, just little thin glass. Bet there's more glass in an ink vile than in this here jar."

I took it in my left hand, kind of bounced it up and down a couple of times, testing the weight and feel. Then I thanked Mr. Nash and headed for the door.

I'd never seen blackstrap molasses in a jar before. It

was kind of strange stuff. It was black as coal, but when I rolled the jar in my hand, the liquid that stuck to the sides was a light yellow color, almost clear in spots. Then it rushed to join the rest of the molasses and turned black again.

Not paying any attention to what I was doing or where I was going, my sore toe bumped the screen door before I looked up. The sudden pain made me jerk. The jar of molasses almost slipped from my hand. I grabbed it. My heart gave about three heavy thumps inside my chest. Mr. Nash would never forgive me if I busted the jar and all that gooey, sticky molasses landed right in the middle of his doorway.

Concentrating on the jar, I made sure I had a good hold on it, then stretched out my little finger to the handle of the screen door. The turkey bell jingled above me. Still staring at the blackstrap molasses, I slipped through the opening and onto the boardwalk.

Best take one more look at that shotgun, I thought. Still staring down at the jar, I turned. But before my eyes could leave the jar in my hand and search out the place in the Mercantile window where that beautiful shotgun was . . .

I ran smack into something. The sudden jolt bounced me back a step or two. I squeezed the jar tight. Once I was sure it wasn't going anyplace, I took my eyes from it and brought them slowly upward, to see what I'd hit.

There were brown shoes. Not really shoes, more like boots. The leather was rough and they were tied with thin strips of rawhide. Brown pants bloused out above them, just below the knees. There was a belt, not of leather but of bright red- and yellow-striped cloth. A blue cotton shirt. Long black hair that draped about the shoulders. A face.

A round face with high cheekbones. A pitted, wrinkled face. It was brown and weathered as a coat left out in the rain and sun for years. A hard face—angry and unmoving. And eyes . . .

It was the eyes that made my breath stop in my throat. They were black eyes—deep and dark as night itself. Eyes that didn't look at me . . . instead, they cut clean inside me . . . clean through like I wasn't even there.

I blinked a couple of times. Tried to make the air go down into my lungs. It was like something was stuck in my throat. My breath held half in, half out, and it wouldn't move.

Suddenly my eyes flashed. I knew the face. I'd seen it before. I'd seen it in newspapers that guests at the hotel left in their rooms. I'd seen the face on the front of a dime novel that Nate Ferguson snuck into school once. It was the face of . . .

Geronimo!

CHAPTER 4

I reckon there are some things in a fella's life that he just don't have time to think out. Sometimes he just has to *do* something—then when it's over he can think about it afterward.

It was kind of like the first time I fell out of a tree. On the way down I didn't think that I should have grabbed another limb instead of the one I did. I didn't think about being more careful the next tree I climbed. I didn't think about not crying 'cause all my friends might laugh and make fun of me.

I just fell. I fell and waved my arms and kicked my feet, and didn't think about anything—not until after I hit.

I guess that's the way it was when I first met Geronimo.

One second I was smiling—thinking about not dropping the molasses and dreaming about having that wonderful shotgun.

The next second I found myself staring up into the dark, glaring eyes of the most fierce, bloodthirsty Indian chief that ever roamed the American West.

Geronimo was so close I could almost feel his breath on my face. My heart stopped. I felt my mouth flop open as I stood there, frozen. Like a statue, I couldn't even tremble, much less turn and run.

Geronimo was too close. There wasn't time.

Then I caught a movement out of the corner of my eye. Someone was behind me!

A hand caught my shoulder. It clamped down. Held me!

Indians! a voice screamed inside my head. *Run! They've got you—fight for your life or—*

There was another Indian. Younger, more slender, he seemed to appear from nowhere to stand between me and the fierce Apache. I was caught! Surrounded!

Something snapped inside me.

Like some wild animal fighting for its very survival, I sprang into action. The jar in my left hand flew straight up into the air. I let go of the sack on my right shoulder. With both hands free, I spun on the man who had grabbed me from behind. I knocked the hand from my shoulder. Threw myself against my attacker with all my might.

Fists pounded into the man's stomach. Feet and knees flew, pounding, driving into the hard bone of shin and kneecap. I fought for my life. Fought off the savage who came with Geronimo to kill me.

The man I pounded fell backward. I felt the sudden jolting stop when he crashed into the wall of Ben Nash's store. A cloud of brownish-gray burst and swirled about me. Like a fog it seemed to swallow me. I coughed, gasping for air. I couldn't see.

Suddenly another man grabbed me. I felt strong hands wrap around my waist. Kicking and yelling, I felt my feet leave the ground as I was lifted.

I kicked, squirmed, twisted. His hold was too tight. I couldn't shake free!

Still, I lashed out. I jerked to free one arm. Aimed my elbow where I hoped the man's head would be.

My aim was true.

I felt the point of my elbow smack against the hard bone of a cheek. A sharp whimper of pain was so close, it hurt my ear. The hold loosened about my waist.

The instant my feet touched the cold wood of the boardwalk, I squirmed around. Hard as I could, I drove my fists into the man's soft stomach. Like my first attacker, this one fell back from the fury of my blows.

Run. You're free. Run!

Only I couldn't. I couldn't see. Frantically I rubbed at my eyes. They felt gritty, like they were filled with sand or powder. I blinked and rubbed again. There was light.

Run! the voice screamed inside my head once more. I ran . . .

It was like bouncing against a brick wall. Even as fast as I was running, when I crashed into it, nothing happened. It didn't budge an inch. I kind of bounced back. I blinked again. My eyes fluttered and finally I could see.

I could see the mean, angry face of Geronimo.

Before I could get my senses—before I could go on the fight again, he had me.

Strong hands clamped about both my wrists. He held my arms, pinned to my sides. He lifted me that way until my feet were off the ground and my face was almost touching his.

It was all over. As strong as the man was, I realized I couldn't struggle free. Geronimo could break me right in half—like I was nothing more than a tiny, dry tree branch to be snapped by an angry wind.

Then . . . suddenly . . . Geronimo smiled. It was a tiny smile. A smile that only twitched the very corners of his mouth. For only an instant it made his mean, angry face seem almost gentle.

Those strange black eyes never left mine. His voice was soft—smooth flowing like the sap from a maple.

"Stop, now." He leaned his face closer, so only my ears could hear. "You are brave warrior. You have won your battle. But they are many. Stop fight now, or they will turn your victory to defeat."

Then he winked and set me back on the ground.

The sound of footsteps came to my ears. Boots running on the boardwalk—heavy, pounding footsteps that grew closer.

A man ran past Geronimo to glare down at me. He wore a blue uniform and hat with a thin yellow cord around it as a hatband. His eyes were almost glazed.

"What the devil's wrong with you, boy?" he

shrieked. "What you go tearin' into my men like that for? You crazy or somethin'?"

I took a step back, escaping the angry finger he shook right under my nose. Still puzzled and confused, I rubbed my eyes once more and glanced around. A soldier sat against the front of Nash's Mercantile—at least, I think he was a soldier. It was hard to tell because his blue uniform was almost solid brown. He rubbed at the back of his head where he had crashed against the wall. Another man picked himself up from the dusty street. He brushed at the yellow stripe on his pants. Dazed and confused, he picked his hat up from the ground and brushed the brown powder from it as he looked around.

"I ought to skin your hide!" the man in the clean uniform yelled. "Fact I think I will." He raised a hand to slap me.

Before I could duck, before I could even blink, another hand shot out and grabbed the soldier's wrist. The brown, weathered hand froze the soldier's blow in midair. He pulled against it, but it wouldn't budge. His head snapped around to see who had him.

When Geronimo's black eyes burned into him, the man stopped yanking to get loose.

Geronimo spoke. Only this time I couldn't understand the words. The soldier frowned.

"You know I can't understand Apache. Let go. You're hurtin' my wrist. Where's that danged interpreter? Blamed Indian ain't never around when I need him. Sontoc?" he blurted. "Sontoc! Where the heck are you?"

"Comin' as fast as I can, Captain Eggers."

The young Indian I'd seen beside Geronimo earlier rushed from the crowd of onlookers. I guess I'd been so busy with things close to me, I hadn't noticed the huge crowd that stood in the street and on the boardwalk all around us. The young Indian was covered from head to foot with the brown whole-wheat flour. He looked like a gooey, sticky ghost as he waddled and sloshed to stand next to the captain.

Another lump came up in my throat. I remembered the jar of blackstrap molasses in my hand. I remembered the sack of flour on my shoulder. I had no idea what had happened to them when I was fighting for my life—no idea, until now.

When Geronimo saw him, he let go of the soldier's wrist and put his hand over his mouth. There was no sound. But beneath his hand, I could see his face stretch tight. His black eyes sparkled like stars in the night sky. Finally a little snort escaped through his nose. He moved his hand from his mouth.

Seeing his smile, Captain Eggers gave a little laugh. I could hear the people around us. Like a contagious cold, they seemed to catch the laughter and pass it from one to the next. In fact, the only ones who weren't laughing were Sontoc and myself.

The young Indian raked spread fingers through his long, black hair. He looked at the gummy mess of molasses and flour that came off in his hand. Then he held it out to me.

"You drop this?"

"Yes, sir. I . . . I . . . didn't mean to. When I seen Geronimo . . . I . . . I thought . . . I . . . er . . ."

He shook his head. "Never mind." Then he turned to the soldier. "You call me, sir?"

The captain nodded toward Geronimo. "What'd he say?"

Sontoc asked Geronimo something in Apache. Geronimo's face strained, then he answered.

"Geronimo say, 'Soldiers not much good fighters,' " Sontoc translated. " 'Young warrior beat up two grown men and still ready for more fight.' "

Captain Eggers kind of bristled at that.

"All they was doin' was fixin' to ask him to move out of the way so we could pass. Whoever figured that crazy kid would light into 'em like he done?"

Geronimo pointed at Sontoc and the corners of his mouth lifted, ever so slightly. He took a deep breath and seemed to force the mean, angry look back to his face before he spoke again.

"Well?" Captain Eggers cocked an eyebrow at the interpreter.

Sontoc looked downright disgusted at Geronimo, then he turned to the captain.

"Geronimo say, 'Young warrior even do better job beat up Indian.' He say, 'Use different tactic, but do more damage than he do to soldiers.' " Sontoc raked more of the gooey molasses and flour from his hair and listened as Geronimo continued. "He say, 'Geronimo free man. No like reservation.' Then say, 'Now maybe Geronimo change mind. With young warriors like this one' "—he motioned toward me—" 'Geron-

2 6

imo think maybe safer to stay on reservation this time.' "

Frowning, Captain Eggers sort of cocked his head to the side. Then he sighed, not knowing whether to believe what he was hearing or not.

"Well, you tell Geronimo that I certainly hope he does. It'd make it a lot easier on all concerned if he'd stay at Fort Sill this time and . . ."

Geronimo folded his arms. No trace of the tiny smile remained on his stern, angry face. With a grunt, he strolled toward me.

"Home," he whispered with a jerk of his head as he passed. "Go quick."

Before the captain could even ask, Sontoc said, "Geronimo say, 'We go now!' "

For a second I almost smiled at the angry-looking savage. Instead, I quickly turned and squeezed through the crowd. I raced down the boardwalk, circled behind Nash's Mercantile, and headed home as fast as I could. The laughter from the people in the crowd followed me. It chased me, and no matter how fast I ran, I couldn't escape it. When it caught me, it rode my shoulder like a heavy weight on my back.

CHAPTER 5

I heard the footsteps coming. I felt his presence when he stepped around the side of the barn. I didn't look up. I was too ashamed and embarrassed.

"How come you hidin' out here behind the chicken coop?" Daddy asked.

I shrugged, but didn't look up.

"Your mama's been callin'."

I took the little piece of wheat straw I'd been chewing on from my mouth. Gently as a butterfly landing on the petal of a flower, I flicked some dirt into the doodlebug mound between my bare feet. A few grains of sand rolled down the side of the cone-shaped depression. The doodlebug flipped them back out.

Daddy stepped beside me. I could hear the boards on the chicken coop creak when he leaned against them to slide his back down the wall and sit.

"Reckon if you was trying to find a place to hide from the whole world," he said, "you'd at least find a place that smelled better. Stinks out here by this old chicken house."

I glanced up for only a second, then went back to concentrating on the doodlebug.

Daddy sat there for a long time. Finally he reached over and took the little straw out of my hand. From the corner of my eye I watched as he wiggled some dirt into a doodlebug hole between us. Nothing happened. He flicked some more dirt. At last there was a little wiggle beneath the surface at the bottom of the cone. A tiny tuft of dust exploded. Daddy waited a moment, then knocked more dirt down the sides.

"It's not as bad as you think," he said, looking at the doodlebug like he was talking to it instead of me.

"Yes, it is! It's probably worse than I think." I folded my arms. "Done went and made a fool out of myself in front of the whole town. I don't even know what happened. I saw Geronimo and . . . and . . . I busted Mama's molasses and dropped all that flour . . . and . . . I'll never hear the end of it. Nate and Cotton and all the rest of the guys at school will never let me live it down. I been tryin' to get a job. Now nobody will even bother to talk to me 'cause of what I done. I made a total mess of everything."

Daddy chuckled. I shot an angry glance in his direction. He clamped his lips together. A little snorting sound came out, anyway.

"Sorry," he said, catching his breath. "Just thinking about the mess. That poor Indian kid . . . it'll take him a week to get all that molasses and flour off. And them two army boys didn't fare much better. Think they were more embarrassed than hurt. You sure whopped 'em good."

I shook my head and glared down at the doodlebug hole between my feet. Daddy sighed, then reached over to take my chin in his hand. His touch was rough and there was black around and under his nails from the grease of the big locomotives he worked on in the roundhouse up in Chickasha. He made me look at him. His smile was soft, yet almost proud.

"But like I said, it ain't as bad as what you think."

"Yes, it is," I argued.

"No."

"But I made a fool out of myself and . . ."

He let go of my chin. I frowned and cocked my head to the side. Daddy smiled.

"You might have felt like a fool, but by the time Geronimo and the Apache left, you come out more like a hero."

"Huh?" I scrunched my eyebrows and my head tilted the other direction.

"That's right." Daddy nodded. "You should have stuck around a while."

"Why? What happened?"

Daddy folded his arms and leaned back against the chicken coop.

"After you lit out for home, things settled some and we made our way on down the street to Spivey's Livery where the army wagon was waitin'. The soldiers got Geronimo and the other two Apache who escaped with him all loaded on the wagon. We were waiting for Edgar Spivey to hook up a buggy, 'cause there were two newspaper reporters going with them that they hadn't counted on.

"Well, you know how people are—curious and all about Geronimo? I guess the whole bunch of us had kinda been inchin' our way closer and closer to get a better look at the old Indian. They was just about ready to pull out when, all of a sudden, Geronimo leaped up from where he was sittin' in the back of the wagon. I mean, that old man just flat-footed it from where he was and landed on the wagon seat beside this young soldier.

"He let out this loud scream. A war whoop, I guess. Shoot, it sent the chills scampering all over me. Then he ripped his shirt off and leaped right smack-dab into the middle of the crowd.

"People commenced to screaming and yelling and running into each other. It's a wonder some of the little kids didn't get trampled. I mean, it was like watching a covey of quail—folks exploded in all directions. Children was wailin', women was cryin', even grown men was whimperin' and shakin' in their boots. I run, just like the rest of 'em. When I stopped to look back, about five soldiers was surrounding Geronimo, aimin' their rifles at him. The old devil just stood there, daring them to shoot."

I was leaning so close, my shoulder was almost against Daddy's. I nudged him with my elbow.

"Then what happened?"

"Well, when we got our nerve up enough to sort

of start gathering back toward the wagons, Geronimo strolled over and climbed on the wagon again. He called the interpreter . . . ah . . ."

"Sontoc," I said, remembering the boy's name.

"Yeah, Sontoc," Daddy repeated. "Anyhow, Geronimo waved for him to step up there, too. I can't remember exactly what he had the boy say, but what it added up to was that us white people tremble at the name Geronimo because he's such a great warrior. He said that when they think he's a prisoner, they act real brave. But when he surprised them, like he surprised you—well, everybody already knew how they ran."

"Then what?"

"Then Geronimo said that the way he saw it, everybody in the whole town was a coward, except for you. He said you were the only one with the courage to face him and try to fight instead of running away like the rest of us done. Then he set himself down in the wagon and wouldn't say no more or look at nobody. Finally the soldiers drove off. Took him back to Fort Sill. Think you made yourself a friend today. And from what I've heard, Geronimo don't have much respect for many white folks, much less consider them friends. You ought to be right proud, Will."

In a way I guess I was proud. In another way it wasn't like that at all. I hadn't been brave. It wasn't a matter of courage. I was just flat scared—so scared I didn't even know what I was doing.

I tried to tell Daddy. He listened and acted as if he understood. He said that sometimes it doesn't matter *why* a fella does something; the only thing that counted is that he *did* it. Then Daddy made a grunting sound as he struggled to his feet. He rubbed his knee a moment, then reached down and helped me up.

"At any rate, there is some good that come of all this."

"What?" I asked.

When Daddy smiled, his chest kind of puffed out.

"Well, I know you been wanting that shotgun in Ben's window, and . . ." He hesitated, pausing so long that it made my insides almost beg to hear what he was going to say.

"And?" I urged.

"And Timmy Locke, the guy who works for Edgar Spivey, over at the livery . . ." He paused again.

"What about Timmy?" I pestered.

"Well, he up and quit day-fore-yesterday. Took off for California. After what happened with Geronimo, Edgar said he might have a job for you."

My eyes popped so big I thought they were going to bust clean out of my head.

"Driving the supply wagon?"

Daddy nodded. Then he held his hands out, to keep me from jumping on him and hugging him around the neck.

"Ain't for certain, and I don't know how much he's planning to pay ya. Another thing, word up in the roundhouse at Chickasha is that they're puttin' in a spur line to the fort pretty quick."

"Spur line?"

"Yeah. Rock Island is fixin' to lay track between Rush Springs and Fort Sill, pretty quick. You do get the job and it may not last too long. At any rate, you're supposed to go down to the livery stables, first thing in the morning, and talk to Edgar."

I knew I was might-near grown. Still, I couldn't help myself. I wrapped my arms around Daddy's middle and hugged him so hard I almost broke his ribs. He hugged me back. Then with his arm around my shoulder and my arm around his waist, we headed inside to help Mama with the evening chores.

CHAPTER 6

Edgar Spivey twirled the tip of his handlebar mustache between his thumb and forefinger. He frowned.

"Well, the army pays me the going rate per trip. 'Course that's payin' for the mules, takin' into account the wear 'n' tear and upkeep on the wagon, *and* me payin' the driver. I was givin' Timmy Locke sixty cents a day. Now be it understood, he was full growed and an experienced mule whacker to boot. You, on the other hand, are twelve and ain't got no experience. I figure thirty cents a day ought to be plenty."

My insides were twitching and jerking. I wanted to yell, "Yes, sir, I'll take it!" But I didn't. Instead, remembering back on what Daddy said at the supper table last night about Edgar Spivey being an "old horse trader" and not respecting anybody who didn't haggle or argue with him, I frowned back and kind of chewed on my thumbnail like I was figuring on my own.

Edgar let go of one end of his mustache and reached over to twist the other end. Finally I took my thumb from my mouth and folded my arms across my chest.

"Way I got it figured, I'm gonna be doin' a man's work. It won't take me that long to catch on, 'cause I learn stuff pretty quick. Sixty cents a day sounds like fair pay for doing a man-size job."

Edgar Spivey let go of his mustache. He folded his arms like I did and glared at me. After a moment his face seemed to soften.

"You're young and strong, Will. It'd be stretchin' things some, but I might could go forty cents. If"—his burly eyebrows arched—"if you feed the mules and clean their stalls after each trip."

Holding my right elbow in my left hand, I stroked my chin thoughtfully. Forty cents was more money than I ever dreamed of. I frowned and slowly offered him my right hand.

"Make it fifty cents and you got yourself a driver."

Mr. Spivey looked at my eyes, then down at the hand I offered. It was all I could do to keep my hand from trembling and shaking clean off my wrist. I forced it to be still. Waited. Ever so slowly a smile curled beneath his handlebar mustache. He grabbed my hand and shook it so hard I felt the bones inside crackle and pop.

"Deal!"

My feet never touched the ground from the time I left Spivey's Livery until I got to school. It was like

floating on a cloud. The sound of Miss Potts's school
bell, usually an irritation, came to my ears as sweet as
Christmas bells today. While Miss Potts read with the
little kids out of the old McGuffey reader, I opened
my Mohan's *Sea Powers*. Only I didn't read it like I
was supposed to. Instead, I looked at the pages and
dreamed of hunting with that beautiful shotgun. I
dreamed of bringing quail and dove and passenger pigeons home to fill Mama's table. I was just about to
shoot an enormous, fat tom turkey when I heard:
"Will? Will!"
Startled, I jerked and looked around. Miss Potts
stood right beside my desk. She glared down at me.
"Er . . . ah . . . yes, ma'am?" I stammered.
Her eyes were tight. Her voice had an edge when
she said: "Hope you had a nice trip. I don't know
where you've been, but I suspect it was not on a sea
voyage with Mohan, nor here in my classroom."
Helplessly I shrugged and tried to smile up at her.
She smiled back, only it was more like a sneer. Quick
as a snake's tongue, she smacked me across the knuckles with the ruler she always carried. I jerked my hand
from my desk and wrapped my other hand about it.
"The chair." She pointed with her ruler. "Put the
hat on as well. Perhaps next time you will keep your
place and read when called upon."
The whole class laughed as I obediently trotted to
the tall stool in the corner. They laughed louder when
I sat down and put the tall paper cap with the word
DUNCE written on it atop my head. Miss Potts made
no effort to quiet them. Instead she laughed, too. After

a time she brought the class to order and continued calling the older kids to read.

It was a small price to pay for not attending to my classwork. My knuckles didn't throb long, and sitting in the "dunce chair" gave me time to shoot the big tom turkey and bring it home for Mama. We were just about to sit down at the dinner table to enjoy our feast when another round of laughter brought me from my daydream.

Looking like a whipped puppy, Molly Price rubbed her knuckles and walked toward where I sat. I hopped up and handed her the dunce cap.

I'd been so busy daydreaming, I didn't hear what had happened. I didn't really need to, though. Molly wasn't very good at reading big words, and Mohan's *Sea Powers* was full of big words. At any rate she was now in the dunce chair, and I had to return to my desk. Somehow, I managed to pay attention, keep my place, and read when Miss Potts called on me, clean up until lunch.

The kids who rode their horses in from the country got their sack lunches from Miss Potts' desk and scurried for the shade of the cottonwood tree behind the schoolhouse. The rest of us, the ones who lived in town, headed for home.

Cotton, Nate, Argus Jacobs, and I always walked together for two blocks. At Main Street Nate and Argus would turn left. Cotton and I went right—him to the store and me to the hotel. I thought about waiting until Cotton and I were alone to tell him about my new job and how I could get the shotgun. But I couldn't hold it any longer.

Cotton seemed right pleased for me. Nate just sneered.

"You won't last," he scoffed. "Won't be no time at all until you quit or get fired and don't have a job no more."

Cotton eased up between us.

"How come you pickin' on Will all the time, Nate?" he said, kind of taking up for me. "He's been wantin' that shotgun since January. He'll stick with the job."

Nate sneered down his nose at Cotton, but his eyes were on me.

"Bet he won't, neither." Nate puffed his chest out, trying to look bigger than he already was. "Injuns is lazy. Everybody knows that. The half-breed here won't last a month 'fore he up and quits. You mark my words."

CHAPTER 7

How come Nate Ferguson hates me? I ain't never done nothin' bad to him."

"Don't rightly know. Some people are just like that."

It was the same answer Cotton had given when I asked him. Mama cut another piece of fresh bread and laid it on my plate next to the bowl of chicken soup. She turned toward the stove, but I caught the edge of her apron and tugged.

"Mama—please, I really don't understand."

Her smile was soft when she turned to face me. She smoothed her apron and sat in the chair next to mine at the kitchen table.

"What don't you understand?"

"He's always calling me a half-breed and saying bad stuff about Indians and pushing me around. If he weren't a year older than me and a whole head taller—

well, Mama, I know you don't hold with fighting, but I'd sure like to—"

"Will." She cut me off by patting my hand and motioning to the plate. "Eat."

"But why is he like that, Mama?"

Mama sighed and leaned back in her chair.

"We've been through this before, son. You're not a half-breed. I am, and I'm not the least bit ashamed of it. My father, your grandfather O'Brien, was Irish. My mother was Sioux. Your grandfather on your dad's side was French and your grandmother Burke's maiden name was Round. That's German. That makes you only one quarter Sioux. Besides your straight black hair and the way you brown up quicker than some of the other boys during the summer—well, your heritage is mostly from Europe."

With my tongue I shoved the piece of bread to the side of my mouth.

"That don't make no difference to Nate," I mumbled.

"Don't talk with your mouth full," Mama scolded.

I heard the gulping sound inside my head when I swallowed the chunk of bread.

"Well, it don't," I repeated. "What's he got against Indians, anyway?"

Mama shrugged.

"It's the way he was brought up, I suspect. Estelle Ferguson is a good-hearted, Christian woman. She never has a cross word for a soul. So I imagine it comes from his dad, Lester."

4 1

I took the spoonful of chicken soup away from my mouth, so I wouldn't talk with my mouth full.

"But why does Lester hate Indians?"

Mama shrugged again.

"No one knows. Your dad heard one time that Lester's father was killed by Comanches in a wagon-train raid. But Marabell Suggens told me that both Lester's parents came from Connecticut and still live over in Arkansas."

"But that doesn't make sense." I cocked an eyebrow, hoping she hadn't noticed the mouthful of food.

"No, it doesn't make sense," Mama agreed. "But it's just the way. Some folks got reason to hate. Other folks simply make up their own reasons. Maybe they really hate themselves. But I reckon hating yourself hurts a powerful lot more than hating somebody else. So maybe they just up and aim all that hate someplace else. In this part of the country, guess Indians are a good place to aim."

She stood up from the table and ruffled my hair.

"Now finish eating and get back to school. You only have to put up with Nate for half a day, then it's Saturday." She paused and tilted her head to the side. "You talk with Edgar Spivey this morning?"

I smiled proudly.

"Sure did. I haggled with him, just like Daddy said. I got me a job and talked him into a good deal."

CHAPTER 8

Some deal," I grumped to myself.

Delilah made a little shuffling sidestep, shying at the muffled *bang* that came from our right. I yanked the reins to get her attention, then popped her across the rump with them to keep her going.

"Some deal," I repeated. "No guests in the hotel this weekend, so hardly any chores to do. Just lay around and rest or could even go hunting with my friends. Instead—look at me—here I sit, on the seat of this wagon, looking at the rump end of two worthless mules and talking to myself. Real good deal I made. Real smart."

On a distant hill to my right I saw Nate Ferguson bring the shotgun to his shoulder. A puff of smoke burst from the barrel. He was so far away that it took a good three seconds for the quiet *bang* to reach my ears. Delilah jerked her head up, but she didn't shy. Cotton Nash was to Nate's left. He rushed toward him. Peter Dutton and Argus Jacobs, who had been off to Nate's right, rushed toward him, too. I watched as Cotton picked up something from the ground and handed it to his friend. Nate stuffed his prize into the back of his hunting jacket, then the four boys separated and disappeared over the hill.

"Probably a quail," I told Samson's tail as it swished back and forth. "They told me they were going quail hunting this Saturday. Cotton even asked if I wanted to come along. But, noooo! I got more important things to do. I got to sit on this wagon and talk to your tail."

Things just hadn't worked out like I'd planned. Fifty cents had sounded like right good pay, and I guess it really was. But the wagon only went from Spivey's to Fort Sill on Saturdays. I'd done the figuring when I got back home, the day I made the deal with Mr. Spivey. My shotgun was gonna cost fifteen dollars, so—if my ciphering was right—the last Saturday in May, the shotgun would be mine.

May hadn't seemed that far off—not back then. But things change. Even time changes, I guess. The clock doesn't move any faster or slower, but the way you *feel* time—that changes.

Used to be, Saturdays flew past. There was hardly time to swim, do my chores, and play with my friends before it was over. Now, with nothing to do but bounce around on this hard wood seat and watch the rear end of two old mules—Saturdays lasted forever.

To make things worse, Argus Jacobs had bought my shotgun. Mr. Nash couldn't order another until the new catalog came out with the prices.

A second *bang* snapped me out of my horrible memories.

"Bet that was Argus," I told Samson's and Delilah's tails. "Bet he got a quail with *my* shotgun."

They didn't care. Bored stiff, I slumped down in the seat. Saturdays lasted forever.

A small farmhouse stood at the base of a hill about a quarter of a mile from the main road to Fort Sill. It was a wood house, whitewashed like the picket fence that surrounded it.

I knew it was Geronimo's house because I had seen him there. Often, I'd see a woman—I guess she was Geronimo's wife—working in the yard or tending a small garden next to the place. A couple of times I'd even seen the old chief himself. It was usually in the late afternoons, on my way back from the fort, when I caught sight of him. He ran and played with children around the elm tree that stood beside the house. I guess the children were his grandkids.

My back ached and my bottom was sore from the time on the wagon seat. Still, I managed a smile when I stretched my neck to look at the house. I don't know why I smiled.

I guess it came from remembering how frightened

I'd been when I first saw the fierce Indian chief in front of Nash's Mercantile. But after I'd seen him helping the woman dig turnips in late October and watched him romp with the little children, I couldn't help feeling a bit foolish for *ever* being afraid of him. I mean, listening to the laughter and watching him dodging and scampering about the yard with a bunch of kids—how fierce could he be?

When I saw no one about, I slumped on the seat once more and popped Samson and Delilah with the leather reins.

"Only five to six more miles," I told their rumps. "Making good time today. Soon as you get me to the fort, we'll unload and you can eat. Might get started back early."

The promise of food or getting home early didn't seem to impress either one of the stupid beasts. They just kept plodding along, never wavering from their steady pace.

Sergeant Thorpe met me when I reined up in front of the headquarters building at Fort Sill. He was a plump, jovial man with a big smile.

"Afternoon, Will," he greeted. "Running a mite early today. It's just three o'clock."

I nodded. "Yes, sir. Made good time." Noting his friendly smile, I couldn't help smiling back. "Not much this trip. Only four boxes in the back."

Sergeant Thorpe came down from the steps and untied the rope at the corners of the oil tarp. He hopped in the back of the platform spring wagon and looked at the boxes.

"One goes right here to the headquarters building," he announced. "Other three go over to the base hospital." He bent down, testing the weight of the boxes. "Tell you what. Go ahead and strap the feed bags on your mules so they can be eating. You carry one of the boxes, and I'll take the other two over to the infirmary. That way you can hurry up and head back home."

"What's the rush?" I asked, wrapping the reins around the break bar. "I don't mind driving over there."

"Big storm coming," he said and handed me one of the feed bags from the back. "Big snow."

I glanced up. It was as clear and pretty a day as I'd ever seen in December. There wasn't a cloud in the sky. I took the feed bag and hopped from the seat. Sergeant Thorpe took the bit out of Samson's mouth and tied the feed bag around his head. I did the same with Delilah.

"Storm?" I asked, looking around once more. "You sure?"

The big man smiled.

"Positive. Geronimo told me so himself."

"You seen Geronimo?"

"Yep. About thirty minutes ago. He was ridin' that black pony of his past here on his way home."

I thought it a bit odd that I hadn't seen him. There was only one road between here and Geronimo's house. I started to mention it to Sergeant Thorpe, but he had already gone around the side of the wagon. While he took one of the boxes into the headquarters

4 7

building, I moved the other three to the tailboard of the wagon and shoved the tarp up next to the wagon seat. When he came back out, he put one box on his shoulder and held the other in one hand. It took both hands for me to lift the heavy wood box from the wagon bed. Struggling, I followed him across the compound.

"Yep," he said over his shoulder. "Old rascal had been into Lawton, boozin' it up. Don't know where he gets his whiskey, but he was drunk as a skunk. If we was following orders, we'd find out where he goes and put a stop to it. But it keeps him quiet and out of trouble. So . . ." He grunted and adjusted the box on his shoulder. "Kind of a shame, though. Back in his day, the old man was a regular legend. Now, ain't nothin' but a sot. Complaining about his arthritis and tellin' 'bout the big snow that's a-comin'. Bet it's sixty-five degrees out and that crazy old coot was bundled up in a big buffalo-skin robe. What a shame."

For some reason I felt a little shame, too. I don't know why. Maybe it was because Mama and Daddy didn't hold with drinking. Maybe it was because I'd seen drunks on the streets in Chickasha and El Reno when we'd taken the train up there. Seen them stagger and talk loud and act real sloppy. Drunks weren't a pretty sight. Or maybe it was because I was one quarter Indian—although I didn't have the slightest idea why that might make me feel the way I did.

I really didn't want to bother thinking about it, so I tried to get Sergeant Thorpe to talk about other stuff. Guess I was hoping the conversation would last a while and break the monotony that would soon come with driving that wagon.

Trouble was, along about dark I was wishing for a little monotony. I wished I was bored and had nothing to think about but watching Samson's and Delilah's tails.

Instead, I couldn't keep my eyes from the wall of dark blue clouds sweeping toward me from the north. It was a solid wall that filled the sky.

A blue northern.

I glanced down. The only thing I had were the two blankets I always carried on the floorboard and that big, lumpy tarp in the back. If the storm was as bad as it looked . . . If it caught me out here on the prairie . . .

I wished I was bored, instead of scared stiff.

CHAPTER 9

Being scared stiff wasn't fun. Being frozen stiff was going to be downright horrible.

Samson and Delilah stopped. I popped them with the reins. They moved on again, one slow, cautious step after another. I wrapped the second blanket about me. Struggling against the fierce wind, I raised up from the bench just enough to tuck the blanket under. Then I fought with the sides, trying to stuff them into the folds of the first blanket so only my eyes and nose were left out in the cold.

It was hard to do. My fingers were stiff. They ached from the cold. The blanket slipped from under my chin and began to flop in the strong wind. I put the reins down and held them under my foot. As soon as I did, the two mules stopped once more. Even with shoes and socks, my feet were already numb. When I wiggled my toes, I couldn't feel them sting anymore. Once the blanket was secure, I got the reins and popped Samson and Delilah. They moved so slowly, the wheels hardly seemed to roll. I sat humped on the seat, clamping my jaws together to keep my teeth from chattering.

I had never felt so alone.

At first the snow had been pretty. Big, wet flakes that sparkled and drifted slowly to the ground. I stuck my tongue out and caught them. The cold light touch made me smile. Cotton Nash had a wooden sled with steel runners. Sunday, after church, we could go to the tall hill out by Saddler Flats. That made me smile, too.

But as night came, the blue northern had blotted out the whole sky. The snow came faster and faster. Ice mixed with the flakes and had begun to sting my forehead and cheeks. I'd taken one of the blankets from the floor and wrapped it tightly about me. Then the wind came. It swirled and whizzed the ice through the air until it felt like pellets from a shotgun blasting my face.

It had stuck to the trees and grass like a heavy blanket of white. It bent the branches beneath its weight. It had bent me, too. Made me tuck up into a tight ball on the wagon seat. Still, the beauty of it—the awesome power—it almost took my breath away.

Now there was nothing even the slightest bit pretty or exciting about the storm. Now I was alone on the open prairie with no one around for miles. I was cold. Colder than I could ever remember. I had no way to build a fire. The only thing between me and the ice and snow and wind were two small blankets. The road was gone. For a time I had been able to see a small depression—the place where no grass grew in the wheel ruts. Now even that had disappeared beneath the smooth solid sheet of white.

Samson and Delilah stopped. I popped them hard with the reins. They took two steps, then refused to go farther.

It was no use. The mules had gone as far as they could. Heads bowed low to keep the stinging slash of the frozen white powder from their eyes and ears, they stood and wouldn't move. Already their backs were covered with ice.

I laid the reins down and wiped a hand across my face. My eyebrows felt heavy, brittle. It was hard to keep my eyes open, and I could feel the ice that covered the tiny hairs on my eyelashes.

Slowly I stood. A shudder of fear raced through me, making my legs buckle. I sank back to the wagon seat.

If there were trees or a clump of brush or even a low spot to hide in, I couldn't see it. If I left the wagon, I might wander for hours in this blinding gale and never reach shelter. Then I remembered the tarp in the back. I could get it. I could wrap myself and . . .

The sigh came from deep down in my throat. With their coarse winter hair and thick hide, the mules would be fine. Me . . . I realized that even with the tarp I wouldn't stand a chance out here in the open. Almost reluctantly, my legs trembling, I stood. At least the tarp would help—for a while. For a time it would break the wind. It would keep more of the wet, stinging snow and ice from wrapping around me like a blanket of death.

My teeth rattled like a drum inside my head. Shivering so hard I could barely keep my balance, I climbed over the wagon seat and reached down.

The tarp was gone!

I knew I had left it right behind the seat, but it wasn't there. Frantic—eyes closed to nothing but tiny slits against the cold—I searched. There—way in the back of the wagon. Somehow, it must have slid or worked its way . . . The wagon creaked and bounced as I walked toward it. I bent down and reached.

The tarp moved!

My hand snapped back like I'd touched hot coals. Chills raced up my spine—chills even stronger than the shivers of cold that shook me. The air stopped in my throat.

I forced a deep breath and shook my head. "It's the cold," I told myself. "You're so cold it's driving you crazy. You're starting to have hallucinations." I caught one corner of the tarp and tugged.

The tarp tugged back!

Again I jumped. My half-closed eyes flashed wide as I stumbled backward against the wagon seat.

The tarp shook. Snow fell from it. Then—slowly—a form rose from the bottom of the wagon.

Like a giant bear, the tarp stood. It loomed above me in the back of the wagon like a huge shadow in the misty white of the swirling storm.

Chapter 10

The tarp spoke!

Now I knew for sure I was going crazy. I was probably frozen stiff and just didn't know that I was already dead. I didn't understand what the tarp said, so like a total fool I asked:

"Huh?"

"I said you are brave and good warrior," the tarp said. "Only not very smart."

"Huh?" I repeated.

The tarp fell to the bed of the wagon. An enormous, black, fuzzy monster appeared beneath it. It was covered with long, coarse hair—like the hide of a cow, only bushy. Two small curved horns stuck out of its head.

"I say, not too smart. Should have stopped wagon in creek bed when snow first start," the hairy monster said.

Hands appeared. They were human hands. They

pushed at the horns and the monster's head came off. A man's head appeared beneath it.

I fell backward. I flipped right over the back of the wagon seat and lay there with my feet sticking up in the air. The hairy monster with the human head moved toward me.

"Not even wear coat. Should have buffalo robe like mine so not turn into big chunk of dumb ice."

Between my feet, I saw the face.

Geronimo shot me a disgusted look and shook his head.

"Trouble with young. Not smart enough to come in out of cold."

Lying there with my back on the seat, my bottom on the backboard and my feet sprawled in the air, I was so scared and confused I couldn't even move when the old man reached out a hand to help me. All I could do was stare at those black eyes and the buffalo robe and feel the snow and ice fill my gaping mouth.

Finally Geronimo took my wrist and hoisted me over the seat back. My knees were so weak I couldn't stand. He held me under my arms.

"Old men feel storm come in bones." The corners of his mouth lifted, just a fraction. "Young man not know much. Just go on about business."

"What . . . how . . ." I stammered.

"Shut mouth before fill up with snow." He gave me a little shake. Once he was sure I could stand by myself, he let go. "Geronimo figure soldiers not think I leave when cold and storm. Good time. While you and sergeant take boxes, I hide under tarp. Send pony home. When snow stop, they come check. See pony in pen and figure old Apache curled up in front of fire. I wait in wagon until you stop to hide from storm. Then slip away. Be free for three or four days before soldiers discover I am gone and come look."

He folded his arms and glared at me. Even through the white of the driving snow, I could see those black eyes. Piercing, angry eyes that seemed to cut straight into me.

"But no! You not stop. Keep popping mules on rump until stuck out here on flat with no shelter." His angry face curled to a smile. He sighed. "Geronimo go, young warrior freeze. Then again, you so dumb, Geronimo not know if such good idea to stay."

For an instant I almost thought I saw a twinkle in those black eyes. He glanced over his shoulder toward Fort Sill. The big buffalo robe rose and fell when he shrugged.

"Geronimo can always run away from soldiers. They just as dumb as young warrior. Guess we stay warm now. Run away some other time."

With one fluid movement he let the robe slip from his shoulders and jumped over the side of the wagon. It was as if he did both things at once. He moved so quick and smooth, the robe was still standing in midair by the time his feet landed on the ground.

"Put buffalo robe inside tarp and get down from wagon."

Still shivering from cold and fright, I kept my eye glued to the man as he walked around the front of the wagon.

"Put robe inside tarp," he repeated.

I frowned. "Why?"

He bent down to pull the wooden pin from the doubletree. "Ever see buffalo?"

"Yeah," I answered. "Seen that little herd they got out by the fort."

Once the mules and their doubletree harness were free from the wagon, he popped them on the rumps with his hand.

"Ever see buffalo when it rains?"

Again I nodded.

He shoved Samson and Delilah forward and left them standing a few steps from the wagon.

"Buffalo always look surly and mean when it rains. Look like mad at whole world. That because buffalo hide soak up water fast as open gopher hole. You not put under tarp where dry, buffalo robe get wet. Be no use to us. We end up cold and wet and mad at whole world like buffalo. Put under tarp!"

I got the robe and put it under the tarp. Geronimo came toward the wagon.

"Now get down."

I felt my hands clench to fists. I didn't know what this savage had in mind, but he'd already let the mules go and now he wanted me out of the wagon.

"Off wagon," he repeated as he reached up for my arm.

I jerked back.

"You stay away from me!" I screamed. "Stay back, you hear!"

The old man looked a bit puzzled. He shrugged.

"Okay. Geronimo not fight you. Too cold." Calmly he walked around and opened the tailboard. Then he moved beside the wagon, near where I stood.

"You sure you want to stay on wagon?"

I didn't answer. I kept my fists doubled, ready to fight.

Geronimo shrugged again.

"Okay."

With that he reached down and caught the edge of the bed. I felt it shake. He groaned, let out a strained grunt as he lifted the side of the platform spring wagon. I grabbed for the seat back to keep my balance. Geronimo groaned again and lifted the side of the wagon higher.

It began to tip. Balanced on two wheels for only an instant, I felt it as it started to flip over.

At the last second I jumped.

I fell clear and went tumbling into a pile of white, fluffy snow. It took a second or two to crawl out of the drift and get my bearings. When I looked back, Geronimo had the wagon turned upside down. The old man walked around it. He shoved the snow with his foot. He knelt from time to time to scoop it with his hands and pile it about the edges of the wagon. Then he started tossing handfuls of snow on the top side. He kept going round and round the wagon until it began to look like a giant snowdrift.

Almost smiling, I moved to help him.

"Buildin' a shelter, ain't you?"

Geronimo ignored me.

I followed him around the wagon. Piled snow with

my foot and scooped with my frozen hands. It was as neat a shelter as you could find. The wagon, turned upside down like it was, would keep the tarp, blankets, and buffalo robe dry underneath it. The way we kicked and packed snow about the edges would keep the cold wind from blowing in through the gaps in the sideboards. The snow we piled on top would add extra insulation from the biting cold.

My hands ached and throbbed. Still I helped him pack the snow. We worked as fast as we could in the blinding blizzard. At last Geronimo stepped back to look at our work. He gave a grunt of approval, then walked back to the tailboard.

"Pretty good tepee," he grunted. "Stay warm and dry inside."

I nodded. Kneeling down, I lifted the tailboard and started to crawl inside. Geronimo stepped in front of me. I looked up at the old man. He shook his head.

"Take shirt, shoes, and socks off first."

I frowned. I didn't go on the fight, 'cause I knew the old chief was trying to help. Still, I didn't like the idea of taking my clothes off out here in the freezing snow.

"Why you want me to take my stuff off?"

Geronimo reached down and took a sleeve between his finger and thumb. It kind of crackled when he squeezed the material.

"Shirt wet. Starting to freeze. Shoes wet. Wagon keep out wind and snow, but not cold. You wear wet clothes, they freeze. Clothes freeze—make you freeze."

I nodded. Numb fingers fumbled with the buttons of my flannel shirt. The cold bite of the snow stung my shoulders and bare back as I flung the shirt aside. Sitting on the back of the wagon, I yanked my shoes and socks off.

Geronimo removed his knee-high, rough leather moccasins and lifted the tailboard. I slipped through the opening and he followed.

Once inside, we had to crawl to move around. There was no room, but still we managed to shove the snow toward the tailboard until we reached the grass beneath it. We put the blankets down first. They were already wet. Then we spread the tarp on top of them and left Geronimo's buffalo robe piled in a lump near the seat. When we had everything smoothed out, and had left a little opening under the tailboard so fresh air could come in, we lay down and pulled the buffalo robe over us.

The thing smelled terrible. I coughed, almost gagging at the sour, rancid stink.

When I breathed through my mouth, it wasn't quite so bad. I lay perfectly still for a long, long time. My arms and shoulders quit shaking and trembling. Finally my toes started to hurt. It was a good hurt. A hurt that told me they were still alive and not frozen. I rubbed my feet together underneath the buffalo robe.

It felt good to be warm. It felt good to know I wasn't going to freeze to death. I was toasty and cozy and safe . . .

Or was I?

CHAPTER 11

The old man had saved my life. Still . . .

As the warmth wrapped about me, my eyelids began to feel heavy. I let my eyes fall shut, for only an instant, before I forced them open. When I was cold, my only thought was survival. Now—warm—my head was empty to think about other things.

I remembered the book Nate Ferguson snuck into school. I remembered reading about the Battle of Casa Grande, where Geronimo and his warriors had massacred a whole regiment of cavalry. I remember how it said that once the soldiers were gone, they had attacked a little settlement. They killed the men and then did unspeakable things to the women and children before they slaughtered them. I could almost see the newspaper headlines that were copied in the book—see the print as clear as if it were written on the insides of my closed eyes:

GERONIMO ON RAMPAGE, AGAIN

Wagon Train Wiped Out Near Phoenix

And another headline that I could see when I turned the following page:

BLOODTHIRSTY APACHE ON WARPATH

Geronimo Murders Settlers Near Yuma, Arizona

As my hand slipped from beneath the buffalo robe to touch my hair, I remembered Chauncy Karlton telling Ben Nash about the ninety-nine scalps on the pole in Geronimo's tepee.

I frowned. Geronimo lived in a white farmhouse with his wife. There was no tepee. He played with his grandkids inside a white picket fence. I wondered if the pole with the ninety-nine scalps was sitting beside the fireplace. I forced my hand back under the warmth of the robe.

"You really kill a bunch of white people?" I whispered. "You really got ninety-nine scalps?"

Geronimo gave a little snort.

"The newspapers and stuff say you've killed hundreds of folk. Maybe even thousands. Is it true?"

There was no sound. I lay for a time. My eyes started feeling heavy again.

"Chauncy Karlton says you got a pole with ninety-nine scalps on it. Says you got it right there in your house so you can look at it and remember killing all them folks. Is it true?"

There was another snorting sound from beside me. I rolled my head, staring at the wrinkled cheek next to me.

"Well, is it?"

Without moving his head, Geronimo looked at me out of one eye.

"You tell people I speak to you in town?"

I frowned. "Huh?"

"When I tell you to stop fight and go home—you tell I speak English?"

I shook my head. "No."

"Not even best friend?"

"No."

"You tell mother and father?"

"No." I shook my head again, remembering. "I didn't tell nobody."

Geronimo's expression never changed. The one eye that glared at me left to stare up at the top of our shelter.

"You tell I speak English, Geronimo never talk to you again. You break secret, Geronimo never help even if you freezing. Understand?"

"Yes, sir. I understand."

The eye blinked and looked back at me.

"You smell buffalo robe?"

My nose crinkled.

"Yes, sir."

The corner of his mouth twitched. Close as I was, I could barely see it.

"Hair from dead buffalo smell bad when wet. Not smell too good when dry. But good for stay warm. Compared to dead person, dead buffalo smell pretty good. Buffalo robe stay on back porch of house unless very cold. Not like way it make house smell."

He stopped talking and just lay there, looking at me out of one eye. Finally, when he didn't say anything, I wiggled beneath the buffalo robe.

"So?" I asked.

He leaned his head and looked at me with both eyes. I couldn't quite describe the way he looked at me, but it made me feel kind of dumb. Finally he sighed and rolled back to look up at the bed of the wagon.

"Why anyone keep little strands of stinky hair on pole? No good to help stay warm. No good for nothing. And, even if did have such a stupid thing, why bring in house when leave nice warm buffalo robe on back porch?"

"Oh, yeah." I sighed. I turned to stare at him once more. "Are you really chief of all the Apache?"

"No."

"But the newspapers—"

"War shaman," he said, cutting me off.

"War what?"

"War shaman. Leader when make raid or have battle. Better than some at read sign and know where enemy is and what they do. White man newspaper never understand. Lazy, too. *Chief* easier word for them to write. Not have so many letters."

"Were you really drunk? You don't act drunk, but

Sergeant Thorpe said you was. Were you really, or just pretending so as you could sneak off?"

"Someday, if you be good friend, I show you."

"You mean tell me."

"Mean show you."

It didn't make sense. You answer a question by telling, not showing. I let my heavy eyes close. It hurt to keep them open. It felt good to close them and rest . . . and relax . . . and . . . I blinked. Forced my eyes wide.

"How come you killed so many people? Was it 'cause the Mexicans killed your first wife and children? Or was it on account of the white settlers were taking away your land?"

"Ask too many questions. Go to sleep."

"Sorry."

I tried to go to sleep, only I couldn't. I stayed quiet and closed my eyes. But when I started feeling cozy and relaxed again, my mouth popped open and the words just came tumbling out. I knew the questions bothered him, so I told him about moving to Rush Springs with Mama and Daddy. I talked about going up to Guthrie last year for the big Fourth of July celebration. I told him about how I got the job driving the wagon and about the shotgun that *used to be* in Ben Nash's Mercantile.

"Go to sleep," he mumbled finally. "Flap mouth so much, let all hot air out. Keep flapping mouth, we have to go outside in snow to cool off."

I shut up. Just as I was about to drift into that dreamy world of sleep, I jumped. I guess I felt like I was falling or something, but I jumped hard enough to wake myself. So I told him about how Samson and Delilah were good mules, only Delilah was scared to death of snakes and how she almost broke our necks once, when she saw one on the road and ran away with the wagon. I told him about Cotton and the other guys at school, and I told him how Nate was always so mean to me and calling me "half-breed" and stuff like that and how I'd tried to fight him once, only he was bigger and stronger than me. I told him how Nate had twisted my arm up behind my back until I cried and how he'd made me say "uncle," and how one of these days when I was bigger and stronger . . .

Even when I heard the old man snoring beside me, I kept right on talking.

CHAPTER 12

I never remembered falling asleep. I woke slowly. I felt my eyebrows arch, but my eyes didn't want to open. My bedroom was cold and the feather blanket felt warm and cozy and . . .

No! The feather blanket didn't feel like my feather blanket. It was rough and hairy. It smelled, too.

My eyes fluttered. This wasn't my room. I blinked again and forced my eyes wide. I found a buffalo robe wrapped tight about me. One hand was out, holding on to my hair.

With a jerk I suddenly remembered where I was. I sat straight up.

My head clunked against the wagon so hard that I fell back down. My eyes crossed and spun around inside my skull for a moment. Already I could feel the knot popping up on my forehead.

"Don't set up quick," a mischievous voice cautioned from beside me. "Bump head on wagon."

I rubbed at the knot and looked to the side. "Thanks."

Geronimo ignored me. With a half smile on his face, he leaned his cheek against the sideboard of the wagon. "Riders come."

The peaceful, almost pleasant look on his old face began to disappear. In its place came that mean, angry look. The face of the fierce Apache I'd first seen when I bumped into him outside Nash's Mercantile. I leaned toward my side of the wagon and put an ear against the icy board.

There wasn't a sound. Nothing.

"Soldiers come, too." He sighed and flopped down flat on his back. "Geronimo old man. Not much good at run away no more. Too slow. Too old."

"If you hadn't stayed to help me . . ."

He glanced over.

"You no tell about our talk?"

"No, sir. Promise."

He winked, then stared up at the top of our shelter. I couldn't help notice the look in his eyes. It was like he was seeing clean through the wagon at the blue sky above. I pressed my ear harder against the cold board. There wasn't a sound.

After a long time, I did hear a voice.

"Here's the mules," someone called.

The voice was close, yet it sounded far away, muffled by the white blanket of snow that nestled about our shelter.

"There's the wagon!" another voice shouted.

Then there was the sound of boots crunching on the hard snow.

"Will? You in there, boy? You all right?"

The sound of Daddy's voice brought a smile to my face. I sat up, careful this time not to whack my head on the wagon.

"Here, Dad! I'm under the wagon. I'm okay."

I could hear them digging away at the snow outside. Then there were sounds of grunts and groans as they dug their fingers under the edge and tried to lift.

"Stay put, Will," Dad's voice came. "Can't lift it. Come on, men. Let's get some of this snow off the top."

There was scratching and scuffling sounds right above my head. A little tuft of snow dropped through one crack and landed right on the tip of my nose. I blew it away.

"Hey," someone barked above me. "There's them boys from the fort. Wave 'em over here to help lift."

In a moment or two I heard Sergeant Thorpe's voice:

"Got your telegram this morning about the boy not showing up. Soon as the snow let off, we come as quick as we could. Just lucky you found him. Sure hope he ain't froze to death and—"

"He's all right," Daddy's voice cut him off. "He's under there and he's okay. He called to us."

"You boys dismount and get over here," Sergeant Thorpe barked. "Hurry up."

I glanced at the old man beside me.

"How did you know?" I wondered. "How did you know the soldiers were coming?"

He didn't answer. He only lay there, staring up. There was no expression on his face, but I couldn't help noticing how his dark eyes looked empty. He blinked and rolled his eyes to look at me.

"You not tell that I talk to you!"

Although his voice was nothing but a whisper, the words came out stern and angry. Quickly I shook my head.

"I won't."

"On three," a voice called. "One . . . two . . . three!"

When the wagon flipped over and they looked under it, all of the men smiled down at me. And about a half second after they saw me and smiled, their eyes sprang open so wide that they looked like eggs frying in a skillet. When they saw Geronimo, they jumped back.

The way they moved reminded me of the time Cotton and I had turned over that rock and found a rattlesnake. They went to pitching and reeling backward. Five or six of them tripped over each other or the thick snow and went piling on top of one another in a clump. Two of the soldiers grabbed for their pistols, ready to draw and fire if Geronimo made the slightest move. Daddy and Sergeant Thorpe didn't jump back or run, but even their mouths flopped open and their eyes got big.

"Geronimo!" somebody screamed.

The old man only lay there, staring off at the crisp blue sky. I crawled out from under the buffalo robe. Daddy rushed to grab me.

"Lord, boy. What's happened to you? Are you . . ."
I hugged him around the middle.

"I'm all right, Daddy. I'm fine. Geronimo saved my life. He kept me from freezing. He made this shelter and . . ."

He pushed me back at arm's length and frowned.

"Your shirt? What—?"

"Got wet while I was driving the team," I explained quickly. "It was already starting to freeze, so I had to take it off. I'm fine."

It took a powerful lot of explaining and talking. Finally I managed to convince Daddy and the rest of the men that Geronimo hadn't hurt me the least little bit. I told them how the old Indian saved my life and how he could probably have made good on his escape if he hadn't stayed to keep me from freezing to death.

"Escape?" Sergeant Thorpe stepped up next to me. "He was trying to escape?"

Suddenly the muscles in my chest felt as if they were stretched as tight as the strings on a hay bale. I cleared my throat and swallowed.

"Yeah, he's all the time escaping. I figured that was what he was doing. It's just a guess." I searched my mind, trying to cover for my friend and not let Sergeant Thorpe know. Then I remembered the sergeant telling me about seeing Geronimo back at headquarters. "That's what I thought, at first," I lied. "Then I got to figuring he was so drunk—remember when you saw him back at the fort? Anyhow, I bet he was so drunk, he saw that flat-bed wagon and the tarp and figured it was his bed at home or something. Bet what really

71

happened is he just crawled up in there and passed out. But—but, if it hadn't been for him, I woulda froze to death, for sure."

Sergeant Thorpe looked down at Geronimo and shook his head.

"Bet you're right, Will. Drunk as he was, you're just darned lucky he woke up and was able to help."

"Darned lucky," I repeated.

The soldiers stayed long enough to help right the wagon. Daddy, knowing I'd be alive but cold, had brought a coat and a change of clothes in his saddle-bags. I dressed as the soldiers put Geronimo on a horse. Two of the soldiers rode double, and while Daddy and Mr. Nash and the other men from Rush Springs hitched up my team, the soldiers and Geronimo headed off for Fort Sill. I climbed up on the seat and looked back at the old man.

As he rode off, he glanced over a shoulder at me. His expression never changed. He didn't smile. He didn't do anything. But for just an instant, my eye caught his. It was all I could do to keep from smiling.

Chapter 13

Except where hidden beneath the shadows of a hill or nestled in the darkness of a deep creek bed, the snow disappeared after three days. The land turned brown and dead-looking again.

When Christmas came, I saw no big rush for saving my money. The railroad had almost finished the spur line from Rush Springs to Fort Sill. Argus Jacobs already had *my* shotgun, and it would take a long time to save up enough for another. Besides, it *was* Christmas!

Daddy had been using a homemade leather strap for his pocket watch ever since his watch chain had broken. The watch was a fine American Horologe from Waltham, Massachusetts. It looked a little silly to carry such a nice watch around on a cheap leather strap. I went down to the Mercantile and bought Daddy a new Dickens chain. It was one with a toggle bar in the middle. Daddy could put his watch on one end of the double chain and attach his watch key from the other. That way everything was right there together. It made a right fine present.

I found Mama a fountain pen. It was a shiny black color, and there was a little gold lever built into the side. All you had to do was stick the point down into the inkwell and work the lever to suck ink up into the pen. It made a nice, modern replacement for her old wooden pen and all those little steel points she kept losing from time to time. Mama squinted and held it out as far as her arms would reach. Then she smiled and looked happy as a lark.

I guess, down deep inside, I was hoping for a shotgun. I got a pair of boots. They were beautiful Wellingtons, black and shiny as coal. Being store-bought, they weren't as fancy as handmades, but I still bet they set Mama and Daddy back a pretty penny. When I took the wrapping paper from the package, they watched my every move. I was right proud of my new boots.

They came in real handy in January. It snowed twice. Although not as fierce as the first snow back in December, the second snow caught me on a Saturday night. I was close to home, but by the time I got in, my feet were the only part of me that wasn't cold and half frozen.

There was an ice storm in late February, but it came during school time. Miss Potts let us out early so the farm kids could make it home before the storm got too bad. The ice was so thick and heavy, it snapped tree limbs and brought the whole town to a standstill for about three days. Even the Rock Island Railroad shut down. It was in February, too, when the rumor started around school that Miss Potts had her a man friend up in Chickasha.

How much truth there was to the rumor was anybody's guess. It did seem as if she wasn't so quick to smack people across the knuckles with her ruler for not keeping their place. Even Molly didn't get sent to the dunce chair quite so often for messing up on big words. It made school a lot more fun.

Come March, she even let Mrs. Ferguson throw a birthday party for Nate. Friday afternoon Nate's mom brought in a big chocolate cake. She also made us put on these dumb-looking little party hats. They were pointed at the top and looked a whole lot like our dunce cap, only much smaller and made of bright colors. We ate cake and got to watch Nate open his packages.

The neatest thing he got was this big, round brown ball. It came from his uncle, way up in New Jersey. Along with the ball came a long letter telling about this new game that was really catching on up in the Northeast. It was called basketball. While the girls, Mrs. Ferguson, and our teacher cleaned up cake crumbs and straightened the room, Miss Potts told us boys we could go out and play the new game. Nate took the letter with the instructions on how to play, and he let Cotton carry the basketball. We tossed the big round ball around while Nate read and frowned at the sheet of paper.

"We need a basket," he announced finally.

"Dad's got some bushel baskets in the back of the store," Cotton called as he tossed the ball to me. "Uses 'em for apples and peaches and stuff."

Nate snapped his fingers and pointed up the street. Cotton trotted off, obedient as a little puppy sent to his doghouse. The rest of us kept tossing the ball back and forth. The tossing didn't last long before it turned into a sort of keep-away game. Without picking teams or anything, we just sort of divided up—half of us trying to get the ball and the other half trying to take it away. Peter Dutton got hold of it and wrapped it tight against his chest. He started running and Argus chased after him, finally getting close enough so he could leap on his back and try to drag him down.

"You guys cut that out," Nate growled. He pointed down at the letter in his hand. "Peter. Says here you can't hold on to the ball and run with it. Got to bounce it to get from one place to another."

"Bounce it?"

"Yeah. And Argus, you can't wrestle with nobody, neither. Got to jump around and wave your arms and stuff, but you can't grab 'em."

Argus's nose kind of curled. "That don't sound like much fun."

He kept reading while we bounced the ball and jumped around, waving our arms and laughing and hollering. Finally Cotton got back with the bushel basket. It was made of thin slats of wood and had wire handles on the side. He handed it to Nate.

Nate put it on the ground beside him and stuck his

foot into it. I heard the snap and crunch as the thin wood slats broke.

"Hey!" Cotton squealed. "That was one of Daddy's good baskets. He wanted it back."

Nate crunched his foot around the bottom of the basket some more. Then he gave Cotton kind of a sneer when he lifted it up. The thing still looked like a basket, only there wasn't a bottom in it.

"You can take it back to him, if you want," Nate scoffed. "But right now we're using it for our basket-ball game."

He folded his letter and stuffed it into the back pocket of his Levi's.

"Now we got to choose sides and have two teams." He turned to Teddy Poston. "Teddy, take them babies over to the tree swing. You guys ain't big enough for this game."

Teddy was in fourth grade and almost as tall as Cotton. He looked at Nate and started to say something, only he didn't. Ace Stephens, a freckle-faced, red-headed kid whose dad had a farm out east of town, darted between Nate and Teddy.

"We want to play, too!"

Ace was only seven. His head barely came to Nate's chest. Still, he was always getting in trouble with Miss Potts for trying to fight everybody in school. He folded his arms and looked up at Nate like he'd spotted a tree he was fixin' to chop down. Nate reached out and put a hand against his chest. With one shove he sent Ace tumbling backward in the dust. Then he turned to Teddy.

"I said beat it. You and the rest of them little kids get out of here."

Ace sprang to his feet. I watched as his face, then his neck, then his bare chest, under the OshKosh overalls that he always wore without a shirt, turned as red as his carrot-top hair. Bare feet stomping in the dust, he started toward Nate. Teddy rushed to him quickly. He wrapped an arm around Ace's shoulder.

"Come on," he soothed. "It ain't no use. He's too big. Come on, let's go swing."

Still struggling to hold Ace, Teddy led the way toward the swings. There were seven other younger boys. They followed in a single line, like a herd of baby ducks following their mother. Heads bowed and feet shuffling in the dust, they made a pitiful sight as they were cast out from our game.

"Okay. Now that that's settled," Nate said and puffed his chest out, "me, Argus, and Cotton will be on one team. Peter, Vance, and Mason—you guys are the other team."

"What about Will?" Cotton asked.

Nate's lip curled. "What about Will?"

Cotton shrugged. "Well, whose team is he on?"

"He ain't. Sides wouldn't be even."

"We could let Teddy play," Cotton suggested. "He's almost as big as we are. That way the teams would be even."

Nate tilted his head so he could look down his nose. "Teams *are* even."

"But . . . but . . ." Cotton stammered.

"No *buts* about it." Nate laughed. "Got to have

somebody hold the basket. Who better than ol' Will Burke?''

Basketball looked like a fun game. There was a lot of running and jumping around and laughing. It seemed as if the more they bounced the ball, the better they got at moving around. Playing basketball looked like a great time.

It was hard to tell for sure, though. When you're standing on a chair, holding a bushel basket over your head against the side of the schoolhouse, you really don't have the right angle on things to tell whether it's that much fun or not.

What was worse, after a while Miss Potts let the girls come out to watch. The younger girls went to play with the boys on the two wood swings that hung from the big limb of the cottonwood tree. A few of them played tag around the outhouse. But Molly, Polly Simmons, and Betty Eden, along with the six other older girls, gathered around to watch us.

Something inside me didn't mind having to stand here like an idiot while the other girls watched—but, for some reason, I hated for Betty to see me doing nothing but looking like a statue with the basket over my head.

Betty's dad worked for the Rock Island. They had just moved to town about the time school started. She was nice and easy to talk to—for a girl, that is. At the church socials we'd even sit together and eat our ice cream. She had this long brown hair and the biggest brown eyes I'd ever seen.

The other girls watched the boys and cheered if the ball fell through the basket and clunked me on the head. Betty watched me with those big brown eyes, and I wanted to be out there playing.

Finally I brought the basket down.

"My arms are getting tired," I said. "Somebody else hold the basket so I can play."

Cotton started toward my chair. Nate stopped him.

"Shut up and raise the basket. I'm fixing to shoot."

I started to raise the basket, then my eyes caught Betty's.

"No. Let somebody else hold it."

Nate threw the basketball as hard as he could. It caught the side of my cheek and bounced my head back against the schoolhouse wall. The chair wobbled beneath me. Somehow, I managed to catch my balance before it tipped over.

"Made me miss my shot." Nate laughed. "Do like you're told, half-breed. Get that basket back up in the air."

I stepped down from the chair and laid the bushel basket beside it. My head was still ringing from being pounded against the wall. Nevertheless, I marched right up to Nate Ferguson.

"You did that on purpose," I snarled.

"So what?"

"So, it ain't right. It hurt."

Nate tilted his head back.

"Poor baby."

"And quit calling me half-breed."

"Or what?"

My fist drew up at my side. I brought it up, level with my shoulder.

"Or I'm gonna punch you right in the—"

I never got the word out. Fact is, the last thing I remembered was seeing a flash of movement. Then Nate Ferguson's knuckles—real close up—right before they landed square on the tip of my nose. Then there was black with these twinklie little stars swirling all around and— Well, it was right pretty—kind of . . .

CHAPTER 14

I saw a horse and rider far in the distance. The pony was small. So was the rider—maybe not small, but short at least. I whacked Delilah with the reins. As we drew nearer, the rider began to take form. He was a heavy man. Big across the shoulders, but short. He was slumped in the saddle, like maybe he was sick or something.

I stiffened on the wagon seat. There weren't many people on this trail. Fact, I hardly ever met anyone. And when you're on the trail—even this close to the fort—it's hard telling what kind of vermin a fella might run across. I held the reins tight, ready to pop leather if the need arose.

The pony was black. The rider had long hair and wore moccasins instead of boots. Head down as if he was asleep, the rider never looked up until he was even with my team.

When he raised his head, I saw an old, wrinkled, angry face. A mean face, weathered by the sun. Lips, cracked and parched from the years of dry, desert wind curled quickly to a tiny smile.

"Hello, Will," Geronimo greeted.

I hadn't seen the old man since that night he saved my life in the storm. I smiled back at him.

"Howdy."

The tiny smile on his face suddenly stretched. For a second I was afraid the cracks on his old parched lips were going to burst wide open.

"Appears young warrior do battle again." He almost laughed. "Nose look like ripe cantaloupe. Both eyes black. Hmmm. Bet it was some fight. Bet other warrior look even worse. Maybe dead, even."

My shoulders went limp. I sagged, dejected on the wagon seat. I couldn't look him in the eye.

"No," I confessed. "I didn't even land one single punch."

The foul stench of sour mash whiskey came to my nose. I peeked up at Geronimo and tried to ignore the smell.

"It was that darned ol' Nate Ferguson again. He's nothing but a bully. Always pickin' on me and everybody else in school."

Geronimo cocked an eyebrow, but he didn't respond.

"I shoulda knowed better." I shrugged. "About two years ago I tried to fight him. He's a year older than me and a bunch bigger. Whooped me all over the place. Guess I just ain't no good at fightin'—but—well, if he weren't so big and—"

"I know what it is like to fight with enemy who is bigger and stronger." Geronimo wasn't smiling anymore. His black eyes looked clear through me. "I remember what it is like. But I have seen you fight. You are brave and strong and quick." He frowned, thinking a moment.

"You take things to fort, then stop by house on way home. Nannan fix good meal. We talk."

He kicked his pony and trotted off.

I hurried on to Fort Sill. I didn't even wait to feed the mules like I usually did. As soon as my supplies were unloaded, I raced back to the little white house at the base of the hill.

The black pony was in a pen beside the barn. There was a chicken coop there and a couple of goats in a pen next to it. No people were around. Near the side gate in the white picket fence was a hitching rail. I took the bits out of Samson's and Delilah's mouths, tied a rope from Samson's neck to the rail, and strapped their feed bags on.

When I still saw no one about, I walked cautiously to the door. The smell of fresh-baked bread greeted me before I even knocked. My knuckles had just rapped the wood frame beside the screen once when the door sprang open. A little girl studied me for an instant, then pushed the screen wide. With a smile she latched on to my wrist and pulled me inside. I followed her through a small living room. There was a rocker by the fireplace, cushioned chairs, and an overstuffed feather couch, just like at home. The next room was a dining area. There was a big oak table surrounded by straight-backed chairs. No places were set and the table was empty except for the red- and white-checkered cotton cloth that covered it.

A woman stood in the doorway to the kitchen. At first I figured it was the little girl's mother—maybe Geronimo's daughter. But the girl who held my wrist lifted my arm so the woman could take my hand. She shook it.

"You must be Will Burke," she greeted with a smile. "My name is Zi-Yeh, but the children always call me Nannan. My husband has spoken of you often. It is a pleasure to have you as a guest in our home." She motioned to the table in the middle of the kitchen. "We've been waiting dinner on you. Come."

Geronimo sat at the head of the rectangular table. He had on a fresh white shirt and had washed the trail dust from his face. There was a flat, Quaker bench on either side. A small boy, a year or two younger than the little girl, sat on the far bench next to Geronimo. A young man I recognized as Sontoc sat beside him. A girl, about my age, was next. The little girl tugged on the cuff of my flannel shirt and motioned to the empty bench on our side. I hesitated.

Sitting down to dinner with a bunch of Apache was something I had never—even in my wildest dreams— seen myself doing. Having Sontoc there, remembering what I had done to him the last time we met . . . well, for some reason I felt downright uncomfortable.

The girl took her place next to her grandfather and patted the bench seat next to her. I glanced down at my feet. They wanted out of there. They wanted back on the wagon. They wanted to run. *You're a guest in someone's home,* I told them inside my head. *You got to be polite. Don't run. Go sit down.*

Once seated, the woman began bringing bowls and stuff to the table. Geronimo gestured to the little boy.

"This is my son, Fenton. You already know Sontoc. . . ." The young man nodded. "My daughter Eva . . ." The girl next to Sontoc was pretty, but awfully shy. She didn't even look up. "Nannan has introduced herself." He reached out a hand to the little girl beside me and ruffled her hair. "This is my granddaughter, Nina. But I always call her Sunshine." His tiny smile broadened. "Because she is my sunshine."

Nannan sat. Except for Geronimo, we all bowed our heads for a moment. When we were through with our silent prayer, Geronimo began passing the food.

It was like sitting down to a meal at home. There were mashed potatoes and green beans. A big basket of fresh-baked rolls with churned butter and a roast. We passed stuff round the table and filled our plates. Just as I picked up my fork and started to pitch in, I noticed Geronimo leaning toward me.

When I glanced up, those black eyes of his seemed to cut into mine.

"Do you know of your mother's name before she married your father? Do you know if her name was Hunt?"

I shook my head.

"No. Her maiden name was O'Brien," I answered. "Why?"

He shrugged.

"No reason. Blue eyes remind Geronimo of someone I meet a long, long time ago. Eat, please."

The mashed potatoes and gravy were fantastic. I cut a piece of roast and put it in my mouth. The meat was even more tender than Mama's roasts. It seemed to disappear on my tongue. There was a little twang to the taste, but it was really good.

"This meat is great," I complimented Nannan after I swallowed. I cut another piece and started to put it in my mouth. "What is it?"

"It is good," Geronimo agreed before his wife could answer. " 'Course," he added, "I always did like that old dog, even if he did bark too much."

Chapter 15

The word *dog* rang in my ears. It was louder and sharper than the ringing from the bell atop the church steeple. The chunk of meat was on the end of my fork and already headed for my open mouth. There it froze, kind of dangling in midair.

My stomach rolled. Cross-eyed, I looked past my swollen nose at it. My arm wouldn't move. The fork wouldn't move. My mouth wouldn't close. There was a growling sound as my stomach rolled again. I thought I was going to gag.

Suddenly a knee whacked mine beneath the table. Still frozen, I didn't move until the pain came again. Somehow, I managed to close my mouth and glance at Sunshine. Her smile seemed to glow as she bumped me with her knee one last time and I leaned toward her.

"He's just funnin' you," she whispered. "It's not really dog. Old Thunder's out sleeping by the barn. He's just teasin'."

The laughter exploded around the table. Even Geronimo smiled bigger than I'd ever seen. I put the fork down and folded my arms. When they finally finished having their fun and started eating again, Nannan nudged me with her elbow.

"Roast beef." She smiled. "I soak it over night in wine. Makes the meat more tender and adds a right nice flavor to it."

When we finished our meal, Nannan and Eva cleared the table. The rest of us slipped outside. Geronimo played tag with Fenton and Sunshine. Sontoc and I sat on a log beneath the old cottonwood and watched them race round and round the big tree. They sprinted far out into the yard and circled the house a few times.

I was so full, I did good just to sit on the log.

"Sure don't act like an old man," I mentioned to Sontoc as Geronimo dodged Sunshine and sprinted off around the house again.

He nodded. "My father said that when he was young, when they lived at San Carlos, they would run maybe fifty to seventy miles in one day. Some of us kids challenged Geronimo to a race one time, back on the reservation in Florida. Probably wasn't more than five miles. He beat every one of us back and wasn't even breathing hard."

After a while Geronimo came to sit beside us on the log. He talked with Sontoc about something that was going on at the fort. I didn't know what they were visiting about, but it involved some man named

Pawnee Bill and a big fair and St. Louis. Whatever it was, it didn't have anything to do with me, so I watched the kids and didn't pay much attention to their conversation.

Finally Geronimo frowned at me.

"You travel much?"

"Just to the fort and back." I shrugged.

"Ever go to St. Louis?"

I shook my head.

He winked at Sontoc. "You go with us, maybe. I fix." He folded his arms and leaned against the trunk of the cottonwood. "Sontoc, keep the children busy for a minute. Will, tell about big nose and black eyes."

I told him about the birthday party and the new game called basketball and how Nate Ferguson made me hold the basket. He kept stopping me and making me back up. He wanted every little detail of what happened and what I'd done. I had to really search my memory to recall all the fine points.

Other than making me back up and repeat stuff, he just listened and didn't say much. Finally he got up from the log and motioned to the west. There was just a bright orange sliver of the sun left, resting atop Mount Scott.

"Your mother and father worry if you too late. Time you go home."

I followed him to the wagon. He took Samson's feed bag off and tossed it in the back. I did the same with Delilah's, then put the bridle bits in both their mouths.

"What do I do about Nate Ferguson?" I asked. "What am I doing wrong?"

Geronimo didn't answer until I was on the wagon seat ready to leave.

"You send telegraph to Nate Ferguson. Give him time to make ready for fight."

I frowned and tilted my head to the side.

"Huh?"

Geronimo looked a bit disgusted.

"Tell me you make fist and bring up by shoulder. Tell Ferguson boy you going to hit him and show you going to hit. This let him hit first. Stop sending telegraph."

"You mean, punch him when he ain't lookin'? That ain't fair, is it?"

Geronimo shrugged.

"Not many Apache. Soldiers always have more guns. More men. Apache not tell bigger enemy when we fight. Wait until enemy not expect battle. Hit enemy, then run away. When they not watch, we hit again and run and hit again. Finally, when enemy same size— we do battle. Apache win many fights that way. You remember."

I didn't really understand what he was talking about, but I sort of had an idea. Maybe after milling it around in my head a while, I could figure it out.

"I'll remember," I promised.

I turned the team and started toward the road. Suddenly I reined them up and looked back at the old man.

"Got one more thing I wanted to ask," I called.

Geronimo walked up beside the wagon.

"Ask."

"Well, sir," I began. "When I met you on the road, I smelled whiskey. A couple of the soldiers who helped unload my wagon was talking about seeing you at the headquarters building and how you were drunk. Only—well—you don't act or talk like the drunks I seen up around Chickasha or El Reno.

"When we were under the wagon, remember? Back during the big snowstorm, and I asked about Sergeant Thorpe telling me you were drunk and—well—you said you'd *show* me. I still don't understand."

"I remember snow. Remember you talk and talk and talk." He paused, looking down the path toward the road. Quiet for a long time, he finally smiled. "You tell me you have good mules except for one afraid of snakes."

He pointed. I looked and looked. Finally, far down the path, almost to where the road from Geronimo's house met the Fort Sill road, I saw it. I could barely make it out. Squinting, I strained my eyes. On top of a flat rock next to the road, I saw the snake.

I was amazed he remembered what I'd said about Delilah being afraid of snakes. I was even more amazed that his old eyes could spot the slimy beast that far away, half hidden on the side of the road.

"Thanks," I said, turning to face him. "Only that don't answer my question about being drunk and . . ."

I stopped, suddenly realizing I was talking to myself. Geronimo had gone back inside the yard. Already he was chasing Sunshine around the old cottonwood and I could hear her laughter.

With a sigh I popped the reins to my mules. I didn't know why Geronimo wouldn't answer me. He seemed so open and honest about things when we talked. Maybe he was embarrassed about being a drunk. Maybe . . .

About a hundred yards or so before I got to the snake, I drew Samson and Delilah to a stop. I hopped down from the wagon and fetched a handful of rocks. Then I started them on again. As we got closer, I began chunking the rocks at the snake. With luck I could scare him off before Delilah saw him and spooked.

I popped rocks all around the stupid thing, and still he wouldn't move. About twenty feet from the snake I had to jump down and get more rocks. Once back on the wagon and sure I had a good hold on the reins, I started chunking again. Finally I hit the stupid thing. I popped him right on the side and scooted him half-way off the warm rock.

Nothing happened. I moved my team closer. Holding the reins tight in my hands, I expected Delilah to bolt any second and take us flying across the pasture.

I blinked. Frowning, I rubbed my eyes. The snake was nothing but a brown stick. No wonder it wouldn't crawl off, I mused. No wonder Delilah hadn't spotted it and gone crazy like she always did.

My head snapped around and I looked back. Geronimo stood, leaning over the white picket fence, watching me. As far away as he was in the evening shadows, it was hard to see. But when I turned he nodded his head up and down, real big. Then he went back with his family.

I didn't understand. I asked him about being a drunk, and he showed me a snake. Only the snake wasn't really a snake, it was a stick and I just thought it was a snake and . . . and . . .

I just didn't get it!

CHAPTER 16

You just don't get it, do you, Will?"

Cotton Nash folded his arms and glared at me. I shuffled my bare feet in the dirt. The summer sun made the earth warm. It felt good to be barefoot again.

"I get it," I answered. "I just don't think it's right, that's all."

Cotton shook his head.

"It don't matter whether it's right or not. You know how Nate is. Me and him get along pretty good. He don't bother me or give me a hard time. But we don't show up, he'll call us chicken and every other name he can think of. He'll get Argus and Peter and all the other guys on us. We'll never hear the end of it."

"But what if Mama and Daddy find out?"

"They won't," Cotton snapped. "Even if they do, so what? Shoot, if my dad finds out he'd take me back behind the woodshed and tan my butt. I wouldn't be able to sit down for a week. Still, that beats having Nate and the rest of the guys make fun of me the whole summer."

He waited for my response. When I didn't do anything but stare at my dusty feet, he turned and headed up the street.

"I don't care what you do," he huffed. "I'm going."

I watched his back as he shuffled away. Cotton's right, I told myself. Nate would make our lives miserable. Still, I argued, drinking and smoking just ain't right. Even if Daddy didn't give me a busting, it would hurt him and Mama if they found out. And they would find out—I just knew it. But if I didn't go with the rest of the guys . . .

Why is it that making decisions gets so much harder the older a fella gets? I don't remember having this much trouble making up my mind between right and wrong when I was little. Cotton was farther away. I looked down at my dusty feet.

Today had been the last day of school. At noon, before Miss Potts rang her bell for us to come in, Nate Ferguson had called us older boys together by the outhouse. Once he was sure none of the younger boys were around, he'd told us that he'd swiped three jars of moonshine whiskey from his uncle's still. They were hidden in the cool-water spring near our swimming hole. When his dad wasn't looking, Nate had also taken a handful of brown stogies from his desk down at the mill. "Gonna have us one heck of a gettin'-out-of-school celebration," he'd bragged, soft enough so no one else could hear. "We're gonna have us one wild party."

My dusty feet shuffled. I glanced up. Cotton was almost to the end of the block. If I went home, my chores were already finished and there was nothing to do. If I ever wanted to fit in with my friends, to be one of the guys . . .

"Hey, Cotton," I called as I chased after him. "Wait up."

A lot of the men who worked on the Rock Island went for a drink after work. Daddy never went with them. He didn't hold with drinking or have much respect for those who indulged. Mama didn't allow drinking in the hotel. It was forbidden.

Even if drinking was forbidden—or maybe because it was—I felt a little tingle of excitement rush through me. My head swirled with anticipation.

The next morning my head was still swirling—only it definitely wasn't from anticipation. It hurt.

It hurt all over!

When I awoke, I was on my stomach. I never slept on my stomach. Spread-eagle on the bed, my hands clutched either side of my feather mattress, and my toes were wedged between my mattress and the wood sideboards of the bed.

Blinking, I remembered how the bed had rocked and rolled and spun around like a tiny ship tossed in an angry storm. Last night I recalled grabbing the mattress

with my hands and feet to keep from being tossed out
of my own bed. My fingers ached from clutching the
mattress so tight. I had to force my hands open slowly.
When I tried to lift my head, it throbbed and pounded
as if someone were beating on it with a hammer. I let
it sink back into the feather pillow, afraid to move.

"Time to get up, Will."

Mama's voice was soft and gentle as always, but it
came to my ears like a piercing scream. I jumped.
When I did, my head throbbed. I pushed it deeper into
the pillow and forced one eye to open.

She stood in the doorway to my room. Arms folded,
frowning, she shook her head.

"Time to get up," she repeated.

I wished she'd quit shouting at me.

"Your breakfast is ready, and you need to get to the
livery and hook up the horse and jump-seat wagon."

Despite the pain, I managed to lift my head.

"Horse and jump-seat wagon?"

She nodded and her frown deepened.

"Your father told you about it last night," she said.
"Although he did say that he doubted you were in any
condition to remember."

"To remember what?" I tried to roll over. When I
did, my stomach ached and tumbled. My head banged
like someone slamming a screen door.

"There is only one box of supplies for Fort Sill, but
you have two passengers. Mr. Spivey sent word yesterday afternoon, when the men arrived on the train. You
are to hitch up the jump-seat wagon, then read the
telegram he has *before* you return here to the hotel and

pick up your passengers. It's almost five-thirty. They're expecting to leave at six, so *get up!*"

I sure wished she hadn't screamed *"get up"* like she did. My head had just stopped pounding. Now it started all over again.

Somehow, I managed to sit up and swing my legs over the side of the bed. The room started to spin, so I rested my elbows on my knees and my head in my hands. For the life of me, I couldn't remember what had happened.

Things had started out well enough. There had been seven of us, counting me. We sat cross-legged on the bank and passed around the quart Mason jars. The clear moonshine tasted horrible. It burned my throat when I swallowed. But with a little goading from Nate and Cotton and the rest of the guys, I managed to get down my share. We talked and laughed and acted downright giddy.

Nate had passed out the stogies and we lit them. The cigars were even worse than the moonshine. The smoke burned my tongue and throat. The thing made me cough and left a horrible taste in my mouth. I drank more moonshine to chase it away. My insides felt light and tingly. I guess the rest of the guys felt the same because we talked and laughed and giggled until we were rolling around on the bank.

But something had happened. I don't remember what or when. I remember that something bad had chased the light feeling away. I remember how the ground started to move and the trees wouldn't hold still when I looked at them. I remembered how my

stomach felt as if it were coming clear up in my throat.
I remember feeling sick—a kind of sick like I'd never
felt before. And I remember hanging over an old rotten log and throwing up until I thought my toenails
were going to come out my throat.

I raised my head from my hands.

"No wonder your stomach hurts," I whispered,
remembering.

I brushed my teeth, dressed, then brushed my teeth
again before I went to the kitchen. Mama put my plate
on the table, then went to serve our hotel guests in the
formal dining room. I sat in my chair and looked at
the food—fatback and two fried eggs.

Mama always sliced the fatback real thin so the
bacon would fry up crisp. The two chunks on my plate
were thick and oozing with fat. The fried eggs seemed
to float in a lake of grease.

I shoved the fatback to one side of my plate, put the
eggs between two slices of bread, and chomped down.

The bark of the old oak tree at the back side of the
outhouse felt cool against my cheek. Feet apart, I clung
to the trunk with my left arm and braced my right
hand on one knee. I rested my head against the rough
trunk so I wouldn't topple over. Despite the odor this
close to the outhouse, I lingered until I was sure there
was nothing left in my stomach to throw up.

"I swear," I promised when my legs were strong
enough for me to stand, "I swear I'll never touch another drop of moonshine as long as I live."

I took a deep breath and headed for Spivey's Livery.

CHAPTER 17

Aside from being a bit top-heavy and wobbly on rough ground, the jump-seat wagon was a lot smoother than the old platform spring wagon. Even so, when we first left Rush Springs, I felt every single bump and bounce—every rut and rock in the dirt road.

The two passengers in the backseat were friendly and polite. I was glad they busied themselves talking with each other instead of with me. Seemed like when I talked, it made my head hurt.

The jump-seat was like a four-passenger surrey, only with a box built over the seat area to keep out the rain and sun. With Shakespeare, Mr. Spivey's prized roan gelding, hitched to the wagon instead of Samson and Delilah, we made good time. It was a little before noon when we passed Geronimo's home. I closed my eyes, envisioning the telegram Mr. Spivey made me read before I left:

SEND WILL BURKE WITH LILLIE AND FAIR ORGANIZER
STOP HE IS NOT TO MENTION OR POINT OUT GERONIMO
HOMESTEAD WHEN THEY PASS STOP EXPECT ARRIVAL
TIME SHORTLY AFTER NOON END

The telegram didn't really make sense. Why would
they specify that I drive the passengers? If they were
going to see Geronimo, why not point out his house?

I didn't really ponder on it for too long. My head
wasn't hurting as bad as earlier, and listening in on the
men's conversation from the backseat was downright
interesting. I'd learned a lot.

First off, the tall skinny man named Phillip Winfield
came from St. Louis. He was some kind of big shot
with the fair they were fixing to have there. A young
man, probably in his early twenties, he reminded me
of a stork. He had a long pointed nose and legs like
I'd never seen before. His spindly legs were probably
longer than Shakespeare's.

The other man was Major Gordon Lillie, Pawnee
Bill. I'd heard of Pawnee Bill before, although I really
didn't know who he was. From the conversation I'd
learned that he used to work for Colonel William F.
Cody—Buffalo Bill—I *had* heard of him. Anyhow, he'd
told the Winfield guy that Buffalo Bill organized his
Wild West Rocky Mountain and Prairie Exhibition
show in North Platte, Nebraska, way back in 1883.
He'd brought Mr. Lillie up from the Indian Territory
to act as an Indian interpreter. Their very first performance was in Brooklyn, New York. A few years back
Mr. Lillie formed his own show. It was called Pawnee

Bill's Historic Wild West Show. He'd told the Winfield guy that it was right hot entertainment in the eighties and nineties, but things were fizzling out a bit since the turn of the century. That's why he figured it was important for him to talk to Geronimo.

Sergeant Thorpe was waiting for us in front of the headquarters building. Even though Pawnee Bill was dressed in civilian clothes, Sergeant Thorpe stood at attention.

"Pleasure to have you at the fort again, Major Lillie," he said, snapping a salute. "Major General Payne is awaiting you in his office. May I show you the way?"

Pawnee Bill saluted back. "I know where his office is. You been behavin' yourself, Jake?"

"Been tryin', Bill." Sergeant Thorpe smiled.

While Phillip Winfield and Major Lillie headed for the door, I got down to get the feed bag for Shakespeare. Sergeant Thorpe took it from me.

"I'll feed the horse and take care of the boxes. You're supposed to stick with them fellas."

I nodded and took the steps two at a time to catch up. Major General Payne was in his office. He greeted Pawnee Bill like an old friend, then shook hands with Mr. Winfield. The stork—I mean, Mr. Winfield—handed him a sealed letter. He offered us chairs and we sat while he opened it and read.

"A letter of introduction from Senator Sparks of Illinois," Payne said. "He requests that Geronimo and some of the Apache be allowed to attend the 1904 World's Fair in St. Louis and participate in Pawnee Bill's Historic Wild West Show." He read farther and

I noticed how his eyes seemed to get bigger around. "Senator says that when he told the president about the intention of the World's Fair Committee, the president seemed to show a special interest in having Geronimo there."

Mr. Winfield nodded.

"You do know Geronimo is expected to ride in President Teddy Roosevelt's inaugural parade. That is, if he is reelected—which I'm sure he will be. I certainly hope the old chief will cooperate."

Major General Payne snapped up from his chair. "We'll do everything in our power to ensure the success of your mission, Mr. Winfield. I'll have a man show you to Geronimo's home immediately."

I'd never seen anybody at Fort Sill hop and scurry around as quick as Major General Payne. Usually things were kind of lazy and slow. Every time I went there, mostly I did a lot of waiting. I suspected it was the letter mentioning the president that got him so excited. It was weird.

Geronimo's camp was even more weird. He lived in a white house at the base of a hill. But when we left the fort, Sergeant Thorpe led us out into the reservation to a small flat at the base of Mount Scott. There, twenty or so tepees stood lining the bank of a stream. I left Shakespeare and the jump-seat wagon under a big oak where Sergeant Thorpe tied his horse. We walked through the camp until we found Geronimo. In front of a tall tepee we sat cross-legged on the ground around a small fire. Sontoc was there, but Pawnee Bill made the introductions in Apache and told Geronimo what they wanted. It was downright strange. I mean, even I knew that the Apache never lived in this kind of tepee. And Geronimo, instead of wearing the OshKosh overalls he usually wore, was dressed in deerskin pants with a loincloth over them. He also had on a long cotton shirt and a blue army coat with lots of buttons. The conversation he had with Pawnee Bill and Mr. Winfield was even stranger than our surroundings.

Geronimo said something in Apache. Pawnee Bill's face kind of went blank. When he leaned his head to the side and didn't say anything, Sontoc leaned toward Mr. Winfield.

"Geronimo say horseless carriage sound like big wind. No such animal."

Mr. Winfield shook his head.

"No, tell Geronimo that the automobile is not an animal. It is a machine. And if he does not believe in its existence, all he need do is accompany us to St. Louis and he may see for himself."

Pawnee Bill still had sort of a confused look on his face. Sontoc turned to tell Geronimo what Mr. Winfield said. It kind of tickled me. I knew good and well the old man could understand every word. And Sontoc, who could speak English as well as, if not better than, I did, seemed to keep stumbling and searching for the right word.

"Geronimo—him want know if can ride on horseless carriage."

Mr. Winfield nodded quickly. "I'm sure that can be arranged. I will personally see to it. But please inform him that he is expected to either ride a horse or walk for the opening ceremonies. The automobile ride will have to come later."

Sontoc spoke, then listened to Geronimo's reply.

"Chief want to know if he can pull reins on horseless carriage. Make go himself."

Mr. Winfield sighed.

"The horseless . . . er . . . automobile doesn't have reins. It has a steering wheel. They are very difficult to control. I seriously doubt that he would be able to drive one on the streets of St. Louis. However, perhaps something can be arranged at the fairgrounds. I can't promise, though."

When Sontoc heard Geronimo's answer, he smiled. I noticed the sly look on Major Lillie's face, too.

"Geronimo say it good you not promise." Sontoc folded his arms. "Him say white man always break promise to Apache. Since you no make big windy promise, maybe he get to pull reins on horseless carriage."

Mr. Winfield cleared his throat. He was being extra polite and nice. Still I could tell he was powerful uneasy about being in the midst of all the tepees and Indians and sitting so close to the fierce Geronimo.

"Could we return to our conversation about the fair?" he asked. "There are a number of details to work out, and we do not have that much time before the fair opens. Please ask Geronimo for his decision."

When Sontoc finished talking, Geronimo just sat there. He glared at Mr. Winfield with that mean look—which he was awful good at doing—then he got to his feet. He stood a moment longer, glaring down at the skinny man with the long legs. Then he grunted.

That was all, just a loud grunt. With that he turned, disappeared into the tepee, and closed the flap behind him.

All of us sat and looked at one another, right puzzled. Finally Mr. Winfield got to his knees and leaned toward Sontoc.

"Did I say something to offend him?"

Sontoc held up his hands.

"Me no know."

We waited. I'd been sitting a long time. I shifted my weight from one cheek to the other. Mr. Winfield squatted on his haunches to wait. He looked awful funny with those long legs folded up under him.

"Most certainly hope I said nothing to offend him," he said.

We looked from one to the other, watched the tepee flap, and waited.

CHAPTER 18

The scream that came to my ears was the most piercing, bloodcurdling sound I ever heard in my life. It was so loud and frightening that it sent the hair standing straight up on the back of my neck. I almost jumped plum out of my skin.

The tepee flap burst open. Geronimo leaped out.

He wore a bonnet draped about his head. The eagle feathers trailed behind, almost touching the ground. Instead of the army coat and cotton shirt, he wore a leather shirt with fringe that dangled from the sleeves and across the chest. He held a tomahawk in one hand and a feathered lance in the other.

Streaks of bright red and yellow war paint lined one cheek. Three other streaks made a lightning shape across his forehead.

Geronimo screamed again, waved the tomahawk in the air, and began dancing.

The frightening sound made my heels dig into the ground. Eyes wide, I pushed myself away from him.

Mr. Winfield was on his knees. Without lifting a leg and rising, one foot at a time, he jumped up. It was like a spring—first both knees on the ground, then both feet. Only when his feet hit the ground, they were moving—and moving fast.

He screamed back at Geronimo. Only the sound that came from his throat was more like a little squeak. Then he ran to his right, back to his left, then off to the right again. After making two or three circles, he took off down the creek bed like a streak. Sergeant Thorpe was hot on his heels, but there was no way he could keep up with Winfield's long, stork legs.

Geronimo watched them with his mouth open. Sontoc looked up at him and sort of shook his head. Pawnee Bill, still next to me on the ground, said something in Apache. He had to repeat it before he got Geronimo's attention.

"Will is friend," Geronimo said, glancing at me. "It okay to talk. What did you say?"

Pawnee Bill gave me a half smile and nodded. Then he turned back to Geronimo. "I said, what was that all about?"

The old man shrugged. "Well, you said to impress him. War paint, bonnet, all the stuff we put on for show in St. Louis."

"Yeah," Bill said. "I asked you to impress him, not scare him to death."

Geronimo shrugged. The tomahawk and lance dangled limply at his sides.

"Whoever figured he'd take it so serious?" A smile came to the old man's face as he watched the two men racing down the creek. "Never seen a white man run so fast."

Already, Mr. Winfield had outdistanced Sergeant Thorpe by a good thirty yards or so. We sat watching the two.

"Must be those long legs." Sontoc chuckled.

I nodded my agreement. "Yeah, he does sort of look like a stork on them long things."

Everybody broke out laughing. Even Geronimo laughed—well, for him it was a laugh. He never made a sound, but his mouth curled up until his eyes were nothing but tiny slits. His tummy bounced up and down as he sank to sit on the ground. We watched and laughed until Winfield and Sergeant Thorpe disappeared around the bend of the creek.

Geronimo took the feather bonnet from his head and tossed it aside.

"Commanche war bonnet smell like dead bird." Legs crossed, Geronimo leaned forward and rested his elbows on his knees. "You work out good deal with people at fair?"

With a shrug, Lillie turned his attention from the empty creek bed, back to Geronimo.

"Yeah. World's Fair is a pretty big deal. They got plenty of cash, but I ain't sure how many of your people we can talk them into. The money's good. You count the pay, four bits each time you sign your name or autograph something, and the button concession . . ." He glanced back at the creek. "Reckon somebody ought to go after 'em?"

"Will and I'll go fetch 'em in a minute," Sontoc answered. "Course, that stork may be clean back to headquarters before we catch him."

We all chuckled again.

"What's a button concession?" I asked Sontoc.

He didn't answer. Lillie cocked his head to the side and frowned at Geronimo.

"By the way, what was that horseless carriage bit about? Shoot, just last year you was toolin' around in one of them cars, here at Fort Sill. Still got a picture of you sittin' in the front seat."

I noticed the little twinkle in Geronimo's dark eyes.

"Things are noisy, but fun." He shrugged. "Thought it be fun to drive one myself. Worth a try."

Lillie just shook his head. "I ain't ridin' with ya."

They commenced talking about the fair and the deal that Pawnee Bill was working on. Geronimo had had Major Lillie tell them that he wanted to take a hundred warriors and his fifty wives. Major Lillie looked around and told Geronimo that Nannan would skin his hide if she heard him making up a story about having fifty wives. Then he laughed and said that Winfield doubted that committee would go for more than fifteen women and twenty or so warriors. We listened for a while and finally Sontoc got to his feet and motioned me to follow.

"We better go after them two 'fore Thorpe runs himself to death."

"What's a button concession?" I repeated as I got to my feet.

"You'll see," Sontoc said, starting for the wagon. As we walked toward the oak tree where Shakespeare was tied, I heard Geronimo say:

"Will, there, wants to go along, too."

I stopped and spun back to face them.

"Don't really have a place for him in the show," Lillie said.

"Find a place."

"Me . . . go . . . ?" I stammered, taking a step toward them.

Geronimo nodded.

"When we eat dinner, you say not get to travel much. Say never been to St. Louis. You go."

I waved my hands in front of me.

"Now, whoa . . . wait. That's been a long time ago. We was just talkin'. I didn't think you were serious. Besides I . . . I don't even know if Mama and Daddy . . ."

"Will Burke go!" Geronimo folded his arms and got that stoic Apache look on his face. "Will Burke no go, Geronimo no go."

"I'll find a place for him in the show," Lillie promised. "Will, I'll talk to your folks when you drive us back to Rush Springs."

Sontoc took my arm. Mouth gaping, I stumbled along as he led me to the wagon so we could go fetch Mr. Winfield and Sergeant Thorpe.

We found Thorpe, still trying to catch Winfield. He was walking and puffing for air. The stork from St.

Louis was about a mile farther. He was still running and didn't stop until I called to him. Where or how far we were from the camp, I don't remember for sure. I was still in sort of a daze. I couldn't believe, from the little conversation we had back in March, that Geronimo remembered and wanted me to go to St. Louis with them.

Me? St. Louis? Me and Geronimo and Apache Indians living in tepees and dressed in Comanche war bonnets? Me?

CHAPTER 19

When you had a good coach—especially one made in Concord, New Hampshire, by Abbott, Downing & Co.—you had the best. Built way back in the 1840s, it was kept shiny and bright as new. Even as six horses raced it at a full-out run, it only swayed and rocked gently as we took the sharp turn.

I braced one foot against the footboard deck. With my left arm laced through the steel bar of the luggage rack for safety, I brought the double barrel shotgun to my cheek. Even as soft as the ride was, it proved hard work to aim over the back of the coach. The sway and rock from our breakneck speed kept the shotgun bobbing up and down. It slipped from my grasp, but I caught it again.

The band of screaming Apache closed on us. The sound of their war whoops filled the air. Again and again, the bark of their rifles cracked the evening stillness.

On the straightaway the coach settled. The up-and-down rock still made it hard to aim, but with no side sway, I was finally able to find my mark. I squeezed the trigger.

The two lead riders fell from their horses. I squeezed the second trigger and the right barrel fired. Two more bloodthirsty Indians hit the dust, as did a third near the back of the racing band of screaming Apaches. This one went down, horse and all in a boiling cloud of dust.

Still I was outnumbered by fifteen to one. I spun, broke the shotgun open, and quickly shoved two more shells into the barrels. When I looked up, the savages swarmed about us like a band of angry hornets. One leaped to the lead horse. I fired. He fell to the rigging and disappeared beneath the thundering coach. Another Apache stood on his Navajo blanket saddle and reached for the back of the coach. I dropped him with the second barrel, and the rider and horse alongside him went tumbling to the ground as well.

Then—they got me!

I dropped the shotgun to the floor of the coach and grabbed my chest. Slumped on the seat, I fell limp against the terrified driver.

This was the end. We were done for.

But . . . *no!*

Suddenly the sound of a bugle came to my ears.

It was the U.S. Cavalry.

They charged to our rescue. Rifles blazing, they seemed to come from nowhere to scatter the ruthless savages like a covey of frightened quail. They only fired their rifles a few times before the cowardly Indians galloped away—fleeing for their lives.

John Carpenter drew the coach to a stop in the center of the arena. Miraculously recovered from a mortal chest wound, I took that as my cue to sit up in the seat and wave to the crowd. The Indians returned, reining their ponies to a stop between the Cavalry and the stage. The dead Indians I'd killed scrambled to their feet.

Truth of the matter was, none of the dead Indians were dead Indians. Despite the coaxing from Pawnee Bill, the Apache who accompanied us thought it was downright stupid to fall off a perfectly good horse. The seven fallen warriors were stunt riders. Making sure their pale foreheads were covered so the crowd could see nothing but the darkened oil-paint makeup on their arms and faces, they trotted out to join us.

Dressed in full western garb, complete with buckskin fringe, Pawnee Bill galloped his chestnut stallion into the arena. He circled once, pulled up in front of the grandstand, and finally waved the crowd to silence.

"Ladies and gentlemen," he called in a loud, echoing voice. "The most terrifying and courageous Indian ever to roam the Old West—the defiant and elusive warrior, who for years, despite every effort of the United States Cavalry, avoided captures—the war chief of all the feared Apache Nation . . .

"GERONIMO!"

My old friend rode into the arena. Complete with Comanche war bonnet and a Cheyenne feathered lance, he galloped his paint gelding only once around the arena. In front of the grandstand he pulled up next to Pawnee Bill. The applause and cheers were almost deafening. Geronimo stared at the people with those black eyes. The angry, hateful, defiant glare never left his face. When the applause began to wane, he and Bill rode one more circle about the arena and we all left.

That's the way it went—twice a day (three if you counted the Saturday matinee)—every day of the week except Sunday. When we finished our spectacular performance, I helped John Carpenter with the Concord coach. We dusted and cleaned every inch of it. Twice a week I cleaned and saddle-soaped the harnesses and riggings while John greased the axles and tightened anything that had worked its way loose during all the excitement. After that it was back to the trains.

At the far corner of the St. Louis fairgrounds there were eight spur line railroad tracks. They fanned out in a circle from an open-air roundhouse. Each country who had sent a delegation to the World's Fair had its own train. How many trains there were, I couldn't even guess. We were always so busy, I never had time to count all of them.

Each train consisted of a dining car and a cooks' car, where meals were prepared and served. Then there were Pullmans to house the people who came with their delegations. The trains ranged from the three cars that housed the tiny French delegation to the nineteen cars that belonged to Barnum & Bailey's Greatest Show on Earth. A lot of people worked for that circus—clowns, acrobats, and tightrope walkers—but the railcars also housed the animals. There were lions and tigers. Strange huge beasts called elephants and hump-backed horses called camels. It was quite a sight.

Our Pawnee Bill train had six cars. We were between the group from China and the Swiss. In the open areas between the rails that stretched out like spokes of a giant wheel, carnival or camper wagons were parked. That's where the married folks and people with families lived. Down near the roundhouse were the bathhouses. There were two for the men and two for the women, and they were the darndest things I had ever seen.

In the bathhouses a fella could actually go *inside* to use the bathroom. When you finished you pulled this little cord, and water came rushing down and swept everything away. The white porcelain bowl was clean and sparkling as new. In the bathhouse you could even take a bath without hauling water. There was a separate room with little stalls. In the floor of each stall there was a hole, and on the wall was a brass spigot. All you had to do was pull the cord, and water came pouring out from the nozzle. A little soap and a fella was as clean as new without having to haul so much as one single drop of water. When you were done, you pulled the cord again. More water came spewing out, and water, soap, dirt—everything went out the hole in the floor.

In the mornings after breakfast, when us kids finished cleaning the dining car, we had school there. Our teacher was a young man named David Talltree. He worked for Pawnee Bill but had been away at college for the past few years. Planning to get married soon, he'd left school for one semester to come to the World's Fair and hire on as teacher. He was also the guy I shot off the back of the lead coach horse twice a day. It always scared me to watch him fall between the hooves of the wagon team.

I knew David from Fort Sill. He was half Comanche and one of the best horsemen I ever saw. When I shot, he would fall from the horse and grab the rigging between the lead pair. Somehow he swung his way underneath the rigging, worked his way between all those pounding hooves until he could catch the doubletree and slide under the coach. Once sure there were no riders directly behind and we were running straight, he let go. It almost always worked. In all the shows we had done, he only got stepped on once.

At any rate, I liked having David for a teacher a lot better than Miss Potts. David was real strict. He worked us hard, though he never made us read out loud. He said it was more important to know *what* we were reading than to be able to say the words. When we finished something, he asked a lot of questions— hard questions that made me really think. We had lots of homework, too. But like I said, I liked him and I felt I learned a whole bunch. After school we did the afternoon show. Between that and the evening show, we had maybe three hours to explore the fair.

That's the part I really loved. And since Mama and Daddy had agreed to let me come for only one month, I made the most of my time. Every spare second I got,

I practically ran from one place to the next, trying to take in as much of the St. Louis World's Fair as I could.

There were people from every place in the whole wide world. The French brought hot-air balloons. Dancers came from Siam and China—women who wore beautiful bright silk. There were men dancers from Switzerland. They wore these funny-looking little short pants with suspenders and slapped their legs and feet when they danced. Horsemen came from Canada and England and Russia. David said the Cossack guys from Russia were almost as good horsemen as the Comanche.

Music from all over the world filled the air. Some of the sounds were strange and eerie; others you could downright pat your foot to. Smells of strange and marvelous foods tweaked at my nose and piqued my curiosity. I tried all sorts of stuff. Although I didn't much care for the things from Japan, Korea, and Iceland, the food from South Africa and Italy was downright delicious.

It was during my exploration of the fair that I finally found out what the "button concession" was. Back at Fort Sill I remembered Pawnee Bill telling Geronimo that the pay was good and mentioning something about a button concession. When I'd asked, nobody bothered to take the time to answer.

When I finally found out, it was downright disgusting.

CHAPTER 20

Although somewhat undignified for a man of Geronimo's reputation, the button concession really wasn't what bothered me. The disgusting part was what they did with the proceeds.

Some fifty yards from the grandstand is where they set up the Indian village. It was a strange mixture of Sioux and Comanche tepees that the easterners and folks from foreign countries believed to be authentic Apache. The women wore either beaded dresses of the Pawnee or skirts and blouses that Major Lillie had acquired from the Seminole—these because of their bright colors. The Apache men dressed in everything from Kiowa to Cherokee, looking like a hodgepodge of all the tribes in the Indian Territory.

Geronimo's tepee was near the center of the village. He sat on his buffalo robe before a Sioux lodge. Two soldiers from Fort Sill were assigned to "guard" him. One was an Irishman by the name of McMasters. The other a corporal named Riggs. They took turns standing at attention, with rifle in hand, while tourists came to visit through Sontoc or one of the other men who would speak for the great Apache "chief."

Geronimo wore his moccasins, fringed leggings, and a bright Seminole shirt covered by a U.S. army sergeant's coat. Worn at the end of the Civil War, the coat was what they called a Yellowleg—the name coming from the yellow stripe down the uniform pants. It was Cavalry blue with three bright yellow stripes on each sleeve. Down the center of the single-breasted, waist-length coat were twelve shiny brass buttons.

Word got around the fairgrounds quickly that if one spoke with respect and courtesy to the famous Geronimo, he might be persuaded to sell one of the buttons from his coat.

A shiny brass button from Geronimo's very own coat—a coat captured in a fierce, hand-to-hand battle from one of the bravest army sergeants ever to ride the Old West—was quite a treasure, indeed. He sold them everywhere from two bits to fifty cents each, but only one to a customer.

And never once did he run out of buttons.

That was because while one of the soldiers was standing guard on Geronimo, the other was sitting at a table in a tepee near the back of the camp. Beside him was a box of Army-issue brass buttons that he sewed onto an extra coat as fast as his nimble fingers could run the needle through the thick material.

When Geronimo ran out of buttons on his coat, the guard escorted him on a stroll through the camp. After all, he was old and needed a break occasionally to work the kinks out of his frail bones. They would duck into the tepee, switch coats, and amble back to the buffalo robe to sell more buttons to the greedy tourists, until that coat was empty. Both McMasters and Riggs took turns sewing buttons. It was quite a racket.

In my rush to see everything there was to see at the World's Fair, I never took the time to figure out what they did with all the money. I never even thought about it much. Not until the next to last day before I had to go home.

After the evening performance John Carpenter and I fed and stalled the horses. Flake, the lead gelding on our team, had sprained his leg during the last wild Indian attack. I stayed to help John put liniment on his swollen knee and walk him around the paddock, until we were sure he was all right. It was much later than usual when I left. David Talltree had assigned an extra bunch of homework, and I knew I didn't have time to fool around if I were to get it done by morning.

Besides, the grounds were quiet, almost deserted. The fair had already closed, and most of the workers were back at their quarters. I walked quickly through the Indian village, enjoying the quiet of the evening. Suddenly the sound of loud voices and laughter broke the stillness. I slowed, but kept walking.

Again the sounds came to my ears. Muffled this time

and shushed, the voices made me stop. I tilted my head to one side, listening.

Cautiously I made my way between the tepees toward the back of the village. There were two wagons, the backs together so the dropped tailboards were almost touching. Some men sat on the wagons. They talked in hushed whispers. I eased closer.

With their legs dangling, Sergeant Thorpe, McMasters, and Sontoc sat on one wagon. On the other were Corporal Riggs and Geronimo. Leaning close to the buffalo hide of a Sioux tepee, I hid in the shadows and watched.

Three empty whiskey bottles were strewn on the ground between the wagons. Another sat upright between Geronimo and Riggs. The men passed a bottle back and forth. They drank in big swigs with their heads rocked back, then they handed the bottle to the man next to them.

Sontoc handed the bottle across to Geronimo. The old man sat cross-legged on the bed of the wagon. He put the bottle down and said something. Sontoc laughed. The others shushed him. Then Geronimo picked the bottle up. He put it to his lips and drank and drank and drank. Still holding it an inch or two from his mouth, he shook the bottle until the last drop dripped out.

That's when he tipped over. Legs still crossed, he sort of fell backward until he was lying flat on his back. He just laid there, legs crossed and sticking up in the air.

A roar of laughter exploded from the others. It was all Sergeant Thorpe could do to finally quiet them.

"Hold it down, you guys," he slurred. "We're gonna get caught, you keep making so much racket."

He leaned forward, looking at Geronimo.

"Better get the old coot home," he snorted. "He's so dead drunk, we'll probably have to carry him."

Sontoc kind of slid over the end of the tailboard, like blackstrap molasses sliding over a buckwheat flapjack. He helped Geronimo sit up, then uncrossed his legs for him. Riggs helped him get Geronimo down from the wagon.

The corporal held one arm and Sontoc propped Geronimo up under the other, and together they staggered toward the trains. I followed, moving from shadow to shadow as they stumbled and swaggered their way.

Geronimo, Nannan, Sunshine, Fenton, and Eva lived in the wagon right across from our Pullman car. I squeezed between my Pullman and the dining car to watch. Riggs and Sontoc had trouble getting the old man up the stairs to his wagon. Finally he fell and they couldn't hold him. Sontoc opened the door, and on his hands and knees, Geronimo crawled inside.

"Still got a couple of bottles left," Riggs told Sontoc as they passed where I hid. "Best come help us finish off the booze."

Sontoc shook his head.

"Thanks, but I've had enough. One more drink, and I'd have to crawl home like the old man."

I crouched under the rear platform when Sontoc

went up the steps and into the Pullman. Hiding there, I waited until Riggs staggered off to rejoin his friends before I came out and sat on the iron steps.

There was homework to finish. David Talltree didn't hesitate to use the birch rod if we neglected our studies. But . . . well . . . I didn't feel like going in and working on my lessons. I didn't feel like doing anything. I just sat there.

My stomach rolled. I felt dirty and sick.

And while I sat and glared at the wagon where the old man had crawled through the door on his hands and knees, I knew why I felt so rotten inside.

It wasn't because Geronimo was once a fierce warrior. It wasn't because he was famous or because he was a war shaman or because I was one quarter Indian and felt that his drunkenness cheapened me, somehow. It wasn't because I felt that his position and reputation should make him a symbol of pride and dignity not only to his people, but to all Indians.

I felt rotten and cheap inside because Geronimo was my friend.

I liked the old man. I cared for him. Then to see him drunk—to see him crawl through the door of his wagon on hands and knees—it was almost more than I could stand. I buried my head in my hands. I tried to fight back the tears of shame and hurt that welled up inside.

How long I sat there, I don't know. A sound finally snapped my head from my hands. That's when I saw him.

A man.

He hid beside Geronimo's wagon. I could barely make him out. He pressed his back against the outside wall and crept in the shadows toward the hitch pin at the front.

A tourist, I thought. Perhaps a souvenir hunter left over from the fair crowd. He was dressed like a tourist in a dark broadcloth frock with a vest and broadcloth trousers. He wore a bowler on his head—a little round top hat with a narrow brim. No cowboy, that's for sure, I decided with a smile.

Then a chill crept up my spine and swept the smile from my face. Maybe he wasn't a tourist. What if he was a burglar? He crept like a thief in the night. With Geronimo in his drunken stupor, he was in no condition to protect Nannan and the children. What if the man was a robber?

Suddenly I was on my feet. Three angry strides carried me into the dusty opening between the railcar and Geronimo's wagon.

"What are you doing there?" I demanded in my deepest voice. "You get away from that wagon!"

Quick as a cat, the man turned to face me. I froze in my tracks.

CHAPTER 21

The instant he spun to face me, I realized that my determination to protect Nannan and the children had carried me farther from the safety of the Pullman than I had intended.

I stood frozen, out in the open and only a step or two from the sneaking intruder in the bowler hat.

Half crouched in the shadows, the man put a finger to his lips.

"Shhh," he hissed.

I took a deep breath.

"Don't you shush me." I tried to sound brave. "You get away from Geronimo's wagon!"

"Shut up, Will," an almost familiar voice whispered.

I squinted, leaning into the darkness. Still, I couldn't see.

"I mean it," I forced my words louder. "You don't

get away from that wagon, I'm gonna scream for help. I'm gonna—"

The man reached up and took the brim of the Bowler. When he lifted it, long straight hair fell from beneath the hat and rested on broad shoulders.

"It's me, Will," he repeated. "Shut mouth before wake whole camp."

He took a step toward me so the moonlight would hit his face.

"Geronimo?"

"Shut mouth and come," he whispered. "We talk when not wake others."

I followed the old man through the shadows of the World's Fair grounds. Once clear of the last Chinese Pullman car, he broke into a trot. I ran, following after him. We passed the P. T. Barnum train. A lion roared. Geronimo kept up the steady pace until we were far across the huge open field where fairgoers parked their wagons and automobiles. In a grove of thick willows he stopped and looked back as if checking to see if anyone had followed.

I was puffing and gasping for air. Already I could feel the sweat on my brow and the dampness under my arms. Geronimo wasn't even out of breath.

"Why you not do lessons?" he asked. "It late, why not asleep?"

I started to explain about having to doctor the horse, then seeing him and the others drinking around the wagons. But before the words came out, I put my fists on my hips and glared at him.

"You ain't drunk, are you?" I shook my head, re-

membering. "But I know you were drunk. I seen you
upend that bottle and suck out the very last drop and
I seen Sontoc and Riggs carry you—"

"You see like you see snake in road," he inter-
rupted softly.

"Huh?" I frowned.

"Geronimo show you once. You no see. You no listen. We do one more time. You pay attention."

I walked beside him from the trees and across a dirt
road. We strolled past a line of houses and headed for
St. Louis.

"You ask Geronimo if he really drunk," he said as
we walked. "Geronimo say he remember your mule
afraid of snake and point to road. What you see?"

"I saw a snake. Only, when I got there, it wasn't a
snake. It was just a stick."

The old man smiled. "You see what Geronimo want
you to see. Eyes see stick, but head see snake. You
spend long time throwing rocks at stick. Remember?"

"I remember." I walked a ways farther, then glared
at him once more. "But the bottle. I seen you pick it
up and—"

"You see Sontoc hand me bottle with whiskey. You
see me put bottle down beside me. What else you see
beside me on wagon?"

"Well, Corporal Riggs was sittin' there."

"What see between Riggs and Geronimo?"

I frowned, trying to remember.

"Oh, there was an empty whiskey bottle, and . . ."
My eyes flashed. I stepped in front of him and made
him stop. "You switched bottles, didn't you? You put

one bottle down and picked up the empty one. You just acted like you was drinking, when all the time it was an empty bottle."

Geronimo smiled. He stepped around me and walked on.

"One time, near Chiricahua Mountains, Cavalry send many riders. Apache run and hide for days. Out of food and water. Cavalry get close. Women and children can go no farther. Geronimo send men out into desert. Take army coats we capture many days before in battle and put on Seguro cactus."

We walked past some tall buildings. An automobile chugged and rattled down the street next to us.

"In evening light, wind blow coats. We hide in rocks and warrior blow army horn. We fire rifles, then duck. Cavalry come fast when hear horn and guns. Out in desert they not see cactus dressed in army coats. They see other soldiers chasing Apache. Wind makes coats flop and wiggle like man running. They make line and charge. Chase Apache for miles into desert before figure out. We take food and horses from wagon. Long gone before they come back."

A drunk stumbled from a bar. Geronimo ducked his head so the man couldn't see his face, and we dodged around him and went on our way.

"You don't never drink, do you?" I asked.

Geronimo stopped and leaned against a building. He folded his arms and looked down at me.

"White man bring guns and cannon and many soldiers. Take land from Apache. Put Apache on reservation or in little cage at Fort Sill. Geronimo cannot be free. But even in little cage at Fort Sill, Geronimo free man!

"Heart and mind still free. Heart and mind take Geronimo to see old friends. Take him to roam land and soar to top of mountain with eagle. No one take that from Geronimo. But white man give drink. Say it make life better. It fun and make happy. Geronimo say—I try it. Figure good way to escape reservation. Good way to run away and be free."

"And what happened?" I urged him to go on. I watched his face, his eyes, as we walked. He seemed to drift away to another time and another place.

"Geronimo kill many men. In battle, kill to stay alive. Many good fights. Come home and sing of our victory around the camp. Tell women and children about brave fight. Other times, kill men not so brave. Kill from anger or revenge. Sometimes, kill just to kill. These times, not sing around our fires. Ashamed and not speak of killing."

He stopped and turned to face me.

"Geronimo has done many things in this life. Because of these things many white and many Apache hate Geronimo—others see Geronimo with respect. Love. If they love or hate, it no matter—I am Geronimo! But of all things I do, the thing that bring most trouble to heart was times I try to run away and hide in white man whiskey bottle. Mind not work so good. Head spin. Make stomach sick. Geronimo want to be free man. Soldiers make body prisoner, so Geronimo try to be free in head. Whiskey make heart and spirit prisoner. They cannot get out. Even in cage, Geronimo free man, but when whiskey take spirit prisoner, there is no escape."

He looked clean through me with those black eyes of his.

"Geronimo make his own cage with whiskey. It is a cage I could not leave. When Geronimo get free—he stay free! Never drink." He turned and we started walking again. "You drink, Will Burke. See it in your eyes the day you come to fort with Major Lillie. Never make prisoner of your own mind, Will Burke. Stay free man in heart and spirit. Stay free man like Geronimo."

"I will," I promised. Then I got to thinking about Nate and Cotton and . . . "But what about my friends? I hardly fit in with them as it is. What if all the other guys are drinking and they want me to? I want the other guys to like me and—"

"Why?"

I paused. Tilting my head to the side, I frowned back at him. "What do you mean, why?"

"Why you want other boys to like you?"

"I don't know." I shrugged.

"If you want to be as one with the other boys, you must like them?"

I shrugged. "They're okay . . . I guess."

"They follow the one you call Nate. Is he a brave warrior? Does Nate lead them well? Is Nate someone you look to with respect?"

I shook my head. "No! Nate Ferguson's a total creep. He's a jerk. I don't know why the other guys tag around with him."

"Follow Nate like blind sheep?"

"Yeah. They sure do."

"Then you want to be like blind sheep, too?"

"No."

"Then you want to be like leader—like Nate?"

"No!"

"Then why do you want to be with them? Why does it matter to you what they think? Why care if they like you or not? You are a man of your own, Will Burke. A free man with your own heart and your own spirit. If you are to make a path for yourself in this life, why waste your time worrying what others think?"

It was a question I couldn't answer.

CHAPTER 22

We spent the rest of the night walking and talking our way through the streets of St. Louis. Geronimo pointed out places he had seen before. Hard telling how many times he'd tricked the soldiers into thinking he was drunk so he could escape. But he seemed to know almost every spot we passed.

It was like there was a map in his head—as if he remembered every little detail he had ever seen. He showed me tall buildings and told me the names of the places and what went on inside. He pointed out churches and cathedrals. We talked about his children and grandchildren and about Mama and Daddy, and I even told him how cute I thought Betty Eden was.

As we rounded a corner by a small park, he glanced to the dark sky.

"Sun come soon," he said, as if he was almost sad

that his time of freedom was close to an end. "We must hurry home before we are missed."

How the old man could run like he did, I couldn't imagine. How old he really was was anybody's guess. I was just a kid—young and strong and in the prime of my life. Still, after about a mile or so, he had to stop and come back for me. I was so tired and out of breath, I simply couldn't keep up.

"We go through waterfront. Fast way home." He motioned for me to follow. "Not good place, but maybe no one around this time of morning."

When he felt I had caught my breath, he began to jog again. Even at thirteen my legs were already longer than his. I only stayed with him for about four blocks before I began to fall behind once more. As we left the center of the city and moved toward the river, the tall clean buildings disappeared. In their place were wooden warehouses, then wooden shacks and small homes with dirty, cluttered yards. Finally by the river there were taverns. Even in the fresh morning air, the smell of stale smoke almost gagged me as we passed. I stopped.

Leaning over with my hands on my knees, I looked down at the ground and gasped for breath. After a time Geronimo's broadcloth pant legs and his moccasins appeared in front of me.

"Go ahead," I huffed, not able to lift my head. "I don't want you to get caught. I can make it. Go on. I'll find my way."

"When five or six Apache learn to run. Father send me to mountain and back. If not home by time Mother and Father eat, no eat." He put a hand on my forehead and lifted so more air could get down my throat. "When you get home, you run. Now, we walk."

I followed along, still wheezing and gasping for air. My sides ached, but the spinning in my head and the feeling that I was going to throw up finally passed. I was just about ready to tell him we could run some more when we heard the scream.

It was a high-pitched, shrill scream. The scream of a woman.

I looked at Geronimo. Geronimo looked at me.

The scream came again, from somewhere up the street. This time it was cut short by a sudden *pop* or *whack* sound.

Geronimo moved cautiously ahead of me. Almost holding my breath, trying to quiet my heavy exhausted breathing, I followed at his heels.

There was a man's voice. Loud and angry, it came from nearby. Still, we could see no one on the street ahead of us. At the edge of the building there was an alley. It was barely wide enough for me to step beside Geronimo and see what was going on. A man and woman stood about twenty feet ahead of us, half hidden in the early morning shadows. The man was dressed in a fine black suit. Aside from the wrinkled coat and pants, he looked quite proper. The woman was tall and slender. She had a feather bonnet and wore a sacque coat over her dress. The coat had feathers all down the front of it.

Mouth gaping in shock, I watched as the man in the black suit slapped her. His hand popped against the side of her head, and the feather bonnet fluttered to the ground.

Then a string of curse words spewed from the man's mouth. Coarse, vulgar words that he spun together like a down quilt to fill the morning air.

My eyes widened. I couldn't believe it. For a man to strike a woman—well—it was the most cowardly thing a man could do. Even Nate Ferguson, rotten as he was, would never stoop so low.

The man raised his hand again. But before I could even blink, Geronimo was there. He grabbed the hand. With one fluid motion he twisted the man's arm until he held it pinned against his back. Then, quick as a cat, he shoved the man forward and crashed him into the side of the building next to the frightened woman.

Geronimo let go of the man's arm and stepped back.

"Woman no good at fight. Too small. You such great warrior—try me."

Snarling, with teeth gritted and gleaming in the light like those of an angry dog, the man spun to face Geronimo. He doubled a fist and lunged.

Geronimo stepped aside and grabbed the fist as it whizzed past his face. Again, he twisted the man's arm behind his back and shoved. He slammed him into the opposite wall. This time, when the man's face hit the wood, it was with such force that dust shook loose from the eaves of the building. I could see it puff and drift down from above in the half glow of the morning light. He shoved the back of the man's head so it banged the wall again. Then the old Apache grabbed his thick wavy shock of brown hair to slam his face into the wall one last time.

Only trouble, when Geronimo grabbed the hair—it came off in his hand!

Eyes wide, the old man dropped the hair and jumped back. The man in the black suit was bald, his head shiny as one of the billiard balls down at Skinney's Pool Hall. Unconscious, the bald-headed man slid down the wall of the building. Eyes closed, he sat there facing the wall.

Geronimo tilted his head to the side. Kind of curious like, he looked at the man. He looked at the hair on the ground. He looked at me.

That's when I noticed the little twinkle in his dark eyes. Ever so slowly he bent to pick up the hairpiece. He lifted it from the ground and shook it. Then he smiled.

An Apache war cry has got to be one of the most blood-chilling sounds ever heard by human ears.

It sent the goose bumps racing up my spine. I jumped back.

The woman screamed and ran off down the alley. With her skirt hiked almost to her waist and feathers flopping behind, she's probably still running to this very day.

The man at Geronimo's feet tipped. In slow motion he tilted. Fell over. His head went *thud* on the ground.

Geronimo lifted the handful of hair above his head. He let out another war cry and commenced dancing around in little circles. Waving the hairpiece in the air, he danced and sang to himself until he could stand it no longer.

Then he laughed. Not a Geronimo laugh with the

corners of his mouth tightened until his eyes were nothing but tiny slits. This was a real laugh. A roaring belly laugh that almost shook more dust from the eaves above my head.

It was contagious. I laughed and laughed until I had to hold my stomach and lean against the wall so I wouldn't fall.

Lights began to come on behind closed curtains. A few people came into the street. A man peered down the alley where we stood.

Hairpiece in hand, Geronimo motioned. I raced after him. Down the street, around the corner, and toward the far edge of the fairgrounds, we never stopped laughing or running until we reached the stand of willows.

There, Geronimo sat beneath a tree and waited so I could catch my breath. I was still laughing inside, but quiet now that we were so close to the fairgrounds.

Geronimo tossed the hairpiece into my lap.

"When we lie under snow, you ask if Geronimo really have ninety-nine scalps."

I nodded, remembering, but amazed that he did.

"Apache not take scalps," he said. Then he smiled. "But if did have ninety-nine, this one would make one hundred. You keep as present. Remember Geronimo when you look at."

I smiled back at him and jiggled the hairpiece.

"It's a good present." I kind of chuckled. "And I won't never forget you."

The smile left his face. He glanced down at the

ground, and I noticed that faraway look. His voice was quiet and soft when he spoke again.

"You go home today?"

"Yes, sir."

"You are a good friend, Will Burke. You go home today, but we not come for another month. Geronimo make better present for you when get home. I take in battle from brave warrior. One day I hope to return to son of man I take from. But—Geronimo old man— probably never find son of warrior with blue eyes."

He glanced up at me for only a moment.

"But Will Burke have blue eyes. Some day, I bring present or send with Sontoc. We tell you story of Jesse Hunt. Keep present in hand and use like man would use. Keep story in heart and remember."

I nodded. Uncomfortable with the serious yet puzzling talk, I started to ease to my feet. Geronimo stopped me.

"Before long, Geronimo escape reservation and soldiers again. Only this time Will Burke tell soldiers."

I felt my eyes flash.

"No . . . no, I'd never do that," I stammered.

Geronimo nodded his head and waved a hand to quiet me.

"Yes, you will. I have seen this in a dream. I have seen the vision, and this you *must do.* You will ride to tell the soldiers. They will come and take Geronimo to the fort, but they cannot stop him.

"This time Geronimo will be free."

CHAPTER 23

The dream—the vision—it bothered me. Geronimo's words clung like a cobweb inside my head, and I couldn't seem to shake them loose.

Geronimo got to drive his horseless carriage.

Right before I left for the train, we went to the arena. With his most stoic Apache look, Geronimo climbed onto the seat next to Phillip Winfield. When they started out, he had trouble getting the thing to go. They jerked and bounced around on the seat, looking like a couple of guys riding a bucking bronc.

Once he got it rolling, they puttered round and round the big open arena. Geronimo might have even talked Phillip into letting him drive out on the streets of St. Louis, if he hadn't crashed into the grandstands on their last circle.

Even then, I thought about the dream.

The work crews scurried about to fix the broken boards while Major Lillie drove me to the train depot in his very own automobile. There was an open field, not far from the edge of St. Louis, where I could see the fairgrounds. They were far in the distance. But as I looked back, I remembered his words—his vision. The old man was wrong. It was just a dream. I would *never* tell on him if he was trying to escape. I'd never tattle about him trying to be free.

After the all-night adventure with Geronimo, I was dog tired. I dozed on the train. Didn't wake up until the Rock Island conductor shook me. My head was fuzzy. I blinked and tried to chase the cobweb of Geronimo's dream from my mind.

The conductor shook me again.

"End of the line, boy. You're home."

The 1904 St. Louis World's Fair was the adventure of a lifetime! No boy of thirteen could ever ask for more.

But it was sure good to be home!

I hugged Mama and Daddy until I was blue in the face. We laughed and talked and stayed up half the night 'cause they wanted me to tell them everything.

Pawnee Bill paid his workers at the World's Fair right well. For riding shotgun on the stage and helping John Carpenter with the horses and coach, I had earned a whole dollar a day. A month, not counting Sundays, had given me a whopping twenty-six bucks. I had saved half of it for my shotgun and spent the rest on presents.

Daddy looked a little puzzled when he held up the

short leather pants with the bright suspenders. I told him all about the Swiss Tyroleers, and although he was intrigued with my description, I could still see the strange look on his face. Daddy and I both knew that he could never wear short pants to work or out on the streets of Rush Springs. So, smiling, I handed him the other box. I got him a pair of wool pants to match his gray coat and a plaid tie straight from Scotland.

Mama's face lit up when she opened the box I handed her. Inside were three packages of the finest silk cloth China had to offer. About five yards to each package, the colors were brighter than any rainbow. The vivid patterns swirled and spun in designs that almost seemed to take her breath away. She touched the silk, rubbing it gently between her fingertips. She held it to her cheek. I noticed the little puddle of water at the bottom of her eye. Then she grabbed me and kissed me until I thought I was gonna have to take a towel to my cheek. Then she got to crying.

I asked her what was wrong, and all she'd do is hold the silk material out at arm's length and sniff. "It's just so beautiful." That night, when they thought I was asleep, I snuck down to listen at the bedroom door. That's when I heard how Mama loved the silk and wanted to start making skirts and blouses out of it. Only trouble, her eyes were going bad. Without glasses she couldn't even see to write letters anymore, much less do the tiny stitching that would be required to make the fine silk into clothing. Daddy said something about getting a second job so he could buy her a pair of glasses. I didn't hear all that was said, because their voices got quiet and I figured I'd best sneak back to my room 'fore I got caught.

The next day at school I had to tell all about the World's Fair again. This time it wasn't as much fun as telling Mama and Daddy because I had to stand up in front of the whole class. Miss Tannenberry, our new teacher since Miss Potts had up and married her man friend in Chickasha while I was away, kept asking questions and encouraging me to describe the elephants and camels and stuff like that.

The guys gathered around after lunch and wanted me to tell them about riding shotgun on the stage. Right before we went inside, Betty Eden stopped square in front of me. She looked up at me with those big brown eyes of hers.

"Tell me again about the girls from Siam." Her voice was soft and sweet as honey dripping from the hive. "Tell me about the dancers and the pretty silk clothes."

For some reason I got all twitchy and jittery inside. I had a powerful hard time talking.

When school finally let out, I went to the hotel and got the sock out of the very back of my dresser drawer. All the money I had, I kept hidden there. I dumped it out on the bed and counted. Thirteen dollars from the pay I got at the World's Fair, and nine that I'd saved up from my wagon route to Fort Sill. I counted twenty-two dollars—just like I figured—then I stuffed it back in the sock and headed for Nash's Mercantile.

*   *   *

Ben Nash licked his thumb and flipped another page in the Sears & Roebuck catalog. He frowned and turned the page back the other way.

"Will," he said, finally looking up. "Don't appear that they're making that double-barrel .410 anymore. Closest thing I can find in the book, here, is a twelve-gauge." He shook his head. "Will you look at that. Darned thing costs thirty-two dollars. Prices just gone sky high. I can't believe it."

I looked at the black-and-white picture of that beautiful shotgun in the catalog he tilted toward me. The number below it glared at me in big black print:

$32.00

Ten dollars short, I thought to myself. Spivey's contract with the army had finally run out. There was no more driving a wagon to Fort Sill at fifty cents a trip. Everything went by rail on the spur line. There was no more riding shotgun on the Concord Stage and shooting at wild Indians at a dollar a day. There would be no shotgun. Not this year, anyway.

I guess I should have been devastated—heartbroken.

Instead, a sly smile came to my lips. It was a Geronimo smile—the kind that curled my lips until my eyes were nothing but tiny slits in my head.

I pointed down at the glass-top display case.

"How much for them reading glasses?" I asked. "Oh, yeah," I added as an afterthought. "I need one of them cigar boxes, too."

"Cigar box? Takin' up smokin'?"

"No, sir. Just need an empty box for keepin' something in."

Mama cried again when I gave her the glasses. Daddy said something about how women are silly and just like that, sometimes. He tried to laugh it off. Only that didn't explain the little drops of water that puddled up at the bottom of his eyes.

I just felt good inside. One of these days, probably long after I was married and living on my own, I'd get me that shotgun. Right now, it didn't matter. The good feeling inside was all that counted.

Things settled down some and went pretty smooth, up until February. That's when Nate Ferguson left me no choice but to whip his tail.

CHAPTER 24

Friday, right after school, Nate Ferguson gathered us older guys under the cottonwood. We sort of hung around the swing, talking and visiting until all the little kids and Miss Tannenberry finally left for home. Soon as they were well on their way, he motioned us close together.

"Got us another batch of moonshine," he boasted. "Three Mason jars hid out by Parker's barn. We leave now, we can polish 'er off before dark."

Despite all the throwing up that had gone on the last time, everybody acted right excited and anxious to be on their way. They trotted off, like blind sheep, following Nate down the road. I clung to the rope swing and watched them.

When Cotton noticed I wasn't following, he circled back.

"Come on, Will. It'll be fun. Let's go."

For a second I thought about my crafty old friend. Then realizing I could never pull off drinking from an empty bottle or pretending to be drunk like Geronimo, I shook my head.

"No, thanks," I told Cotton. "Don't hold with drinking. You guys go ahead."

Evidently, Nate noticed that Cotton and I weren't with his herd. He turned.

"What's wrong with you two. Come on!"

"Ah, it's Will," Cotton complained. "He don't want to go."

Nate glared at us.

"What's wrong, Will? Chicken?"

I ignored him and smiled at Cotton.

"Go on with your friends," I told him softly. "I ain't gonna tell on you. Go ahead."

"Come on, Cotton," Nate taunted. "Leave him. He's nothin' but an egg-suckin' half-breed."

The hair bristled across the ridge of my back like the hair on an angry dog. A fist clenched at my side.

"Nate," I snarled. "I'm just about halfway fed up with you calling me half-breed."

Suddenly he rushed toward me. Fists drawn up at his sides, he charged. I held my ground. He stopped and leaned toward me. He was so close our noses almost touched.

"What you gonna do about it, half-breed?" he sneered.

That's when I remembered. I forced my fist to open. Held my hands out, helplessly, and tried to look scared.

"I'm sorry, Nate," I almost whimpered. "I ain't gonna do nothin'. I didn't mean to get you all riled."

Finally Nate got that self-assured, sloppy smile on his face. He turned to Cotton.

"Like I said," he boasted. "Nothin' but a egg-sucking, half- —"

His fists relaxed at his sides. He said *half,* but he never got the word *breed* out of his mouth. The instant I saw his arms relax at his sides, I flew into him.

Hard as I could, I popped him square in the jaw with my right. I swung my left fist up and caught him smack on the tip of the nose. Then I slugged him two more times with my right fist—hard as I could swing.

Eyes crossed, he staggered backward. Nate didn't go down. He blinked and shook his head a couple of times. His angry eyes focused on me.

I took off!

Like a shot, I raced across the grounds and darted around the corner of the school. Behind me, I could hear Nate. His heavy feet pounded the hard ground, packed tight by last night's cold winter rain. He didn't stand a chance of catching me.

That's because I had taken the advice Geronimo gave me when I couldn't keep pace with him back in St. Louis. Every day after school I had run to Ratliff Hill and back. The last two weeks I'd sprinted clean to the top before turning for home.

Once to the school I had to slow my pace so Nate wouldn't lose sight of me. I let him chase me two times around the schoolhouse. I was barely jogging, and he was huffing and out of breath.

After letting him get close enough so he could almost grab me, I sprinted off. I darted around the far corner of the building and stopped. Flattening myself against the wall, I waited.

When I heard Nate's big feet thundering around the corner, I jumped out and raised my knee. My kneecap slammed into his soft stomach. I heard a *whoompf* from him, then he doubled over, wheezing for breath.

I brought both fists down as hard as I could on the back of his neck and took off again.

This time I didn't circle the school. I ran back for the cottonwood. After looking over my shoulder to make sure he was after me, I slipped behind the tree to hide.

Even without seeing him, I knew there was a smile on Nate's face. He had me now. He knew where I was hiding. He would race across the playground and then slowly sneak around the tree—probably from the right since I'd disappeared on the left—and grab me.

Finally here he came.

Creeping like a cat, he eased around the tree. His right hand was open. Poised like a snake ready to strike, he'd reach out and catch me.

Only I wasn't there.

He stopped. Leaned out from the tree to see if I was circling. I waited. It took him so long to run across the playground that my arms were getting a bit tired. My hands ached from hanging on to the limb, right above his head. I held my grip until he finally looked up.

The second he did, I brought both feet down as hard as I could. The high-riding heels on my Wellingtons caught him square on top of the head. Nate Ferguson dropped to his knees. The force of my blow sent a shock wave from the bottoms of my feet clean up to my shoulders.

I let go of the branch and landed lightly beside him. Then I slugged him upside the head again and ran.

I didn't go very far. Staggering and holding his head with both hands, Nate came around the tree. The moment he was in view, I let go with the swing. From above my head I launched the wooden seat at him with all my might. Ropes taut, the heavy chunk of wood flew toward him. His eyes flashed, but it was too late. There was a loud *crack,* then a little scream, when it caught him square on one kneecap.

I wanted to run off again, but I waited. Nate had to be chasing me if it was going to work.

It took forever for him to crawl to his feet. Then, trotting slowly ahead of him, I ran for the outhouse.

Staggering and wobbling, he chased after me. I flung open the door and slammed it shut behind him.

"I'm gonna kill you, Will Burke!" he threatened as he limped toward my hiding place. "I got ya now!"

Through the half-moon hole in the door, I watched. Mud was caked on Nate's upper lip where blood dripped from his nose. His left eye was already beginning to turn blue and swell. His chest heaved up and down. Out of breath and hurt, he stumbled toward me, still roaring his threats.

"I'm gonna rip your head off! I'm gonna get you out of that outhouse if I have to tear the whole thing apart! I'm gonna . . ."

That's when I saw his eyeball peering through the half-moon.

Both hands braced against the door and my feet on the wooden toilet seat, I lunged. I shoved with all my strength.

The door flew wide and smacked Nate Ferguson's face flat against the wood. He staggered backward. I leaped from the outhouse and went after him.

He was a whole head taller than me, so I launched my fists from clean down beside my hips. With each blow, I had to jump to hit him.

First my right fist. Then my left. Another right. My left fist was poised at my side, ready for another upper cut, when I saw his eyes roll back in his head.

His knees didn't crumple. He didn't reach back to cushion his fall. It was like watching a tree toppled by an ax. Stiff as could be, Nate Ferguson fell backward and landed spread-eagle on the ground.

Eyes closed, he just lay there and didn't move.

The other guys rushed up. Mouths gaping in astonishment, they looked first at Nate, then at me.

"You knocked him plum out, Will," Cotton gasped from beside me. "Bet he don't call you half-breed no more."

I started to agree. Then, with a smile, I glanced at the other guys.

"I hope he does," I said, brushing my hands together like I was knocking the dust from them. "That was kinda fun."

*   *   *

153

I left the hotel before sunrise the next morning. Shakespeare was a good horse. He pulled a wagon and his gait was smooth under a saddle. What was better, he was free. Edgar Spivey told me I could borrow him anytime I wanted. I left a note and we took off before five. Shakespeare and I made good time.

I hadn't seen my old friend since the World's Fair. I told him about the fight. I told him how I had fought like an Apache. I hit and ran and hit and ran, until Nate Ferguson was whittled down to my size. No black eye, no swollen nose—not even a single mark on me. While Nate, on the other hand, looked as if he'd had a run-in with a bobcat or something.

Geronimo was right proud of me. He put an arm around my shoulder. "Will Burke make good warrior. Not Apache, but you learn good."

CHAPTER 25

It was also in February, four years later, when I left the hotel before sunrise again. Four long years that had seemed to fly past as quick as the blink of an eye. Four years of growing. Four years of fun times and sad times.

But today I had the most exciting news to tell my old friend. This time my news was much better than back in the winter of 1905. This time there was a girl. Not really a girl, a young lady. Her name was Elgia Baum and she went to business school up in Chickasha. I could hardly wait to tell my old friend that she had consented to be my wife.

I hadn't seen Geronimo for some time. Zi-Yeh, the one we all called Nannan, had died of a tubercular infection the same year as the World's Fair. Mary Loto was a widow and somewhat younger than Geronimo.

Although she was nice, I never felt as comfortable with her as with Nannan. It didn't bother me, nor surprise me much, when they divorced, not long after they were married. I saw him again at Fenton's funeral. I had seen him only a couple of times since then.

The last time I had seen my old friend was when Eva went off to school at the Chilocco Reservation. It had been a long time.

"A long, *long* time," I told Shakespeare. "Shoot, I don't even know his new wife's name."

Still, I could hardly wait to tell him my news. I pushed Shakespeare, but not hard enough for him to break a sweat and get all lathered up. I kept him moving enough so that I reached the little white house at the base of the hill by midmorning.

Mrs. Jozhe, a neighbor who lived on the next farm north of Geronimo's, stood at the corner where the road from the house met the Fort Sill road. I smiled and waved when I saw her. She didn't smile back.

As I neared, I saw the worried look on her face. Frowning, I reined up beside her and hopped down from the saddle.

"What's going on, Mrs. Jozhe? What's the matter?"

"Find black pony, three days ago. Geronimo not with pony."

I smiled and heard a little sigh of relief slip from my throat.

"He's just snuck off again," I assured her. "Bet he's clean to Texas by now and . . ."

She turned and the worry in her brown eyes cut my words short.

"No. Find in stream near black pony. Three days now, he cough and hold chest. Face feel hot all yesterday."

"He's a tough old rascal." I tried to sound light and happy. "He'll be all right. He's just—"

"Not this time!" Mrs. Jozhe said, cutting me off.

I swung to the saddle and dug my heels into Shakespeare's sides. He hadn't even stopped when I slid from his back and raced to the house. A whole bunch of women stood around. I fought my way through the crowd, took one quick look at the pale, almost ghostly figure on the bed, then ran back outside.

Despite the fact that it was mid-February and cold as could be, Shakespeare and I were both lathered up and sweating when we got back with the men from the fort.

When the soldiers lifted him on the stretcher and placed him carefully into the back of the ambulance wagon, Geronimo smiled at me.

It wasn't until that moment that I remembered the dream. His smile told me—the look brought his words back to my mind and to my ears:

"Before long Geronimo escape reservation and soldiers again. Only this time Will Burke tell soldiers."

In my mind's eye I saw us sitting beneath the willow tree at the far corner of the fairgrounds. I saw myself shake my head and swear to him that I'd never do something like that.

"Yes, you will," Geronimo had said. "I have seen this in a dream. I have seen the vision, and this you *must do*. You will ride to tell the soldiers. They will come and take Geronimo to the fort, but they cannot stop him.

"This time Geronimo will be free."

As the wagon raced off for Fort Sill, I felt a tear roll down my cheek. I knew I'd never see my old friend again. Then, a faint smile came to my face. The salty taste of my tears couldn't chase it away. I knew that, at last, Geronimo would be free.

The funeral was a simple affair. The fort commander gave the eulogy and the base chaplain read from the Bible. The Apache women had to go back to the house to wail and cry and sing his death chant. That was because the good Christians at the fort didn't deem it civilized to make so much racket at a funeral.

While the women sat on the floor of the living room, rocking back and forth and chanting, Sontoc pulled me aside.

I followed him to the barn. There, glancing all around to make sure no one was about, he climbed to the hay loft. He came back with a leather bundle about four feet long and a foot across.

"Geronimo wanted you to have this, Will," he said.

"What is it?"

"Open."

I put the bundle on the ground and began unrolling the leather.

A rifle! No, a shotgun! It was plain, with no etching on the metal or carving on the wood stock. It was a lever-action twelve-gauge shotgun. The butt plate was steel, and the stock was pitted and scarred. The barrel, sawed off short, was kept clean and sparkling as new.

A lone eagle feather was tied to the barrel with a strip of rawhide.

I looked up at Sontoc.

He smiled.

"It is not a boy's gun," he said solemnly. "It is the gun of a man. A great warrior. Geronimo took it in battle, and it was one of his most prized possessions."

He motioned for me to follow.

"We will go to the top of the hill. There I will tell you of the one called Jesse Hunt and how, alone, he killed eleven of Geronimo's best warriors and almost ended Geronimo's own life. You will remember the story. You will tell your children of the gun, and they, in turn, will tell their children."

I clutched the shotgun to my heart. I got to my feet and followed him, in silence, to the hill behind Geronimo's house.

EPILOGUE

The old man rocked back and forth. The heavy wood rocker squeaked from time to time. With more patience than he dreamed he would ever have, he watched his grandson scamper about the room.

The little boy of five had blue eyes and shocks of curly blond hair. His pudgy little legs carried him swiftly about the bedroom as he explored first here, then there, then returned to examine places and things he'd already seen.

From the nightstand he lifted a porcelain jar.

"What's this, Grandpa Bill?"

"That's the jar I keep my false teeth in at night," the old man answered.

The boy darted to the open door of the closet. There he dropped to his hands and knees and crawled inside.

When he stood, he pushed aside the bundle of old dusty suits and shirts that hung on hangers.

"What's this, Grandpa Bill?" he said, pointing to the glass door of the gun case. He yanked on the door a few times, but finding it locked, he turned back to his grandfather.

"Can you open it for me, Grandpa Bill?" His eyes seemed to sparkle. "I want to see the big gun. Is it a rifle?"

"It's my shotgun."

"It looks real old," the little boy said over his shoulder. "Did you buy it when you were little?"

Smiling, the old man shook his head.

"No. It was a present that was given to *my grandfather,* Will Burke, a long, long time ago."

"Can you open it so I can see? Can I play with it? Please, please, please."

"No."

"Why, Grandpa?"

"You're not old enough. Someday it will be yours. Someday we will walk to the top of a quiet hill where there is no one else around, and I will tell you of Jesse Hunt and the shotgun. But not now."

The little boy discovered the cigar box, hidden in the closet beside the guncase. He lifted the lid cautiously, then rocked back on his heels when he saw the pile of hair inside.

The old man bit his lips to keep from laughing. Quickly the boy shut the box. He picked it up and scampered across the room, handing it to his grandfather.

"What's this, Grandpa Bill?"

"A scalp."

Blue eyes popped wide.

"A scalp? How did you get it? Where did it come from?"

The old man patted his leg. The little boy climbed to sit in his lap, and they began to rock slowly.

"A long, long time ago there was a brave Apache Indian warrior by the name of Geronimo. Legend has it that he had ninety-nine scalps hanging from a pole in his lodge. If the legend were true, what you see in the box, there, makes one hundred scalps. . . ."

"One hundred scalps?" Blue eyes danced with excitement.

"Yes, one hundred scalps." The old man opened the box so the boy could gaze on the hair as he talked. "Now, sit back and I'll tell you the story. . . ."

ABOUT THE AUTHOR

When BILL WALLACE was a child, his grand-mother told him many exciting stories. Some of these tales involved her own childhood memories of the times she had seen the fierce Apache warrior Geronimo. Will Burke, Bill's grandfather, actually accompanied the representatives of the St. Louis World's Fair when they went to ask Geronimo if he would attend. Bill's grandmother also told him "the legend of one hundred scalps."

Native Oklahomans, Bill and his family consider the settings for this story as familiar haunts. From Rush Springs, where his grandfather drove a freight wagon, to the headquarters building and Geronimo's grave at Fort Sill, they have seen them all.

Bill Wallace's novels have won seventeen state awards and made the master lists in twenty-four states.

.